Biggie
and the
Fricasseed
Fat Man

Biggie
and the
Fricasseed
Fat Man

Nancy Bell

THOMAS
DUNNE
BOOKS

St. Martin's Press ⋈ New York

THOMAS DUNNE BOOKS.
An imprint of St. Martin's Press.

BIGGIE AND THE FRICASSEED FAT MAN. Copyright © 1998 by
Nancy Bell. All rights reserved. Printed in the United States of
America. No part of this book may be used or reproduced in
any manner whatsoever without written permission except
in the case of brief quotations embodied in critical articles or
reviews. For information, address St. Martin's Press, 175 Fifth
Avenue, New York, N.Y. 10010.

Library of Congress Cataloging-in-Publication Data

Bell, Nancy
      Biggie and the fricasseed fat man / Nancy Bell. —1st ed.
          p.   cm.
      "A Thomas Dunne book."
      ISBN 0-312-19238-X
      I. Title.
    PS3552.E5219B5   1998
813'.54—dc21   98-23893
                                                              CIP

First Edition: November 1998

10   9   8   7   6   5   4   3   2   1

This book is fondly dedicated to those who fill my life with joy:
Sara Presley, Anna Presley, Mary Katherine Hughes,
Casey DeNicola Bell, Tara Elaine Bell,
Brian and Jason McAdams,
and Sunday and Trey Sewalt.

Author's Note

The fictional county of Kemp and the town of Job's Crossing, Texas, are bound to remind some of the piney woods of Northeast Texas. However, it must be noted that the town and its wacky residents live only in the author's mind. Don't be fooled into thinking that the characters or events in this book exist outside my own fantasies.

Biggie
and the
Fricasseed
Fat Man

Prologue

The day it rained feathers in Job's Crossing, J.R. and Rosebud were gathering pecans in the front yard. Biggie and Willie Mae sat on the front porch picking them out so that Willie Mae could make pralines and pecan pies for the upcoming Christmas bazaar.

J.R. had just discovered an old skate key on the ground and had turned to ask Rosebud what it was when the sky turned black as night and a blast of wind tore across the yard, stirring up a whirlwind of leaves and almost knocking J.R. off his feet. J.R.'s cat, Booger, who had been resting on a limb, laid back his ears and spat into the wind.

Rosebud laughed. "Be careful, cat, lest you wants to spit in your own eye. Gawd dawg! What was that?"

What it was, was a white feather floating down from the sky. Another feather followed that one, then another, until pretty soon the sky was full of them, whirling and flying all around. In no time at all the ground was as white as if it had snowed all night.

Next door, Mrs. Moody's little white poodle, Prissy, began running around in circles, barking and trying to bite the feathers. Biggie stepped down off the porch and stared at the sky as the wind filled her skirt like a parachute.

"God bless a billy goat!" she said.

Downtown on the square, Butch Hickley polished the show window of his florist shop, Hickley's House of Flowers. He wanted to make sure everyone who passed got a good view of his new Christmas display: white twinkling lights, silver glitter, and masses of angel hair surrounding a moving tableau of the holy family, clad in silver lame robes. The hand of the Virgin rose and fell heavily as it patted the Baby Jesus while Joseph's head rotated from side to side as if to say, *No, no, no.*

"Oooh, that tickles," Butch said as a large white feather drifted past his left ear like a lover's kiss. "Who is that?"

"It ain't no*body*, you miff-minded tenderfoot," boomed Clovis Threadgill, who had just driven up on his riding lawn mower. "It ain't nothing but a derned chicken feather."

At that moment, the new police chief, Paul and Silas Wooten, happened by. "Mr. Threadgill, how many times am I going to have to tell you you can't ride that lawn mower on the sidewalk?" he asked. "I don't want to have to write you another ticket."

Clovis Threadgill drew a toy pistol from the holster strapped around his waist. "Draw, you sidewinder," he said.

Just then, Mrs. Mattie Thripp stepped out the door of

her tearoom. "Snow!" she trilled. "We're going to have a white Christ . . . Oh, Lord love a duck! Norman, get out here this minute . . . and bring the broom!"

Out south of town at the Fresh-as-a-Daisy Poultry Farm and Processing Plant, Firman Birdsong wiped away a tear as he watched a cigar-shaped cloud of feathers being swept away by the wind. He turned grief-stricken eyes toward his brother, Ben, who awkwardly patted him on the shoulder.

"Gone, gone, gone!" he cried. "Fifty thousand dollars. Gone up in smoke . . . er, wind!"

"Brother," said Ben, "how come you didn't put a tarp over them feathers?"

Firman pulled a large red bandanna out of his pocket and blew his nose with a great honk. "I was going to, only I didn't get the time. I had them Mesicans goin' after it this very minute. There they come now." He cupped his hands around his mouth and yelled into the wind. "Ya'll can put it back, now," he called to the three men dragging a huge tarpaulin. "Put-o in the barn-o!"

The men grinned and, shaking their heads, started back in the direction they had come from.

"What am I going to tell those fellers from the duvet company?" he asked. "I promised them a ton of feathers to be picked up this very afternoon."

"Brother, if I was you, I believe I'd give them fellers a call and tell them we'll have their feathers next month. What we got to do now is finish getting ready for the big grand opening of our café," Ben said. "You promised Miss Fairy Lee you'd meet her down there at four-thirty."

The Birdsong brothers, heirs to the family farm, had extended their mother's modest egg business to include

3

chicken and turkey processing, feed, eggs sold statewide, and now feathers to be processed and passed off as goose down. Their success was attributed by the townspeople to Firman's fearless marketing skills tempered by Ben's ability to squeeze a dollar until it hollered. The restaurant, their newest business venture, was dear to Firman's heart. He envisioned a chain of restaurants featuring chicken cooked in every style known to man.

"Brother, have you settled on the menu for the grand opening?" Ben asked.

"The works," answered Firman, his natural ebullience restored. "Broiled chicken, baked chicken, barbecued chicken, chicken and dumplings, sweet-and-sour chicken, chicken croquettes, chicken-fried chicken, chicken and dressing, chicken fricassee . . ."

1

J.R.," Biggie yelled from the top of the stairs, "this is the third time I've had to call you. Are you coming, or am I going to have to come down there and jerk you bald-headed?"

"You better git," Rosebud said. We were sitting at the kitchen table playing battle. "I seen a feller jerked bald-headed once, an' it ain't a pretty sight."

"J.R.!" Biggie hollered even louder.

"Yes'm," I said. Biggie wanted me to get dressed so we could go to the grand opening of the new Fresh-as-a-Daisy Chicken Restaurant and Takeout, which Mr. Firman Birdsong had built out on the bypass.

"Don't wear that shirt," Biggie said, coming into my room without even knocking, "it's got a hole in it."

"Yes'm," I said. You're wasting your breath if you even start to argue with Biggie.

Biggie was wearing her new navy blue dress with the yellow daisies on it. She dug around in my drawer and pulled out my Sunday shirt. "Wear this," she said, giving me a hug, "and comb your hair real nice. Put some water on to hold your cowlick down."

"Can I sit up at the counter with Rosebud?" I asked.

"Nope. Rosebud's taking Willie Mae down to Odie's Place for ribs," Biggie said.

The Fresh-as-a-Daisy Chicken Restaurant and Takeout is painted sky blue and has this great, huge daisy on a green pole for a sign. Mr. Birdsong told everybody it was seven feet taller than the golden arches at McDonald's. When we got there, cars were jammed in the parking lot and lined up on both sides of the street.

"Where you gonna park, Biggie?" I asked. I was afraid she'd try to enter that parking lot, and it would be demolition derby time. Biggie doesn't think much of the rules of the road.

"Over at the Big Eight Motel next door," she said. "They won't mind."

She drove right across the strip of grass that separates the motel from the restaurant and pulled in beside the most amazing car I'd ever seen.

"Golly," I said.

Biggie got out and stood with her hands on her hips, gazing at the car. It was a Cadillac, the kind you see in old-timey movies, the ones with lots of chrome and fins. It was painted orange and white, and, right up front where the hood ornament ought to be, someone had mounted a pair of cow horns; not just any horns, these were longhorn horns. They must have been six feet from tip to tip. I peeked inside and saw that the seats were covered in brown and white cowhide with the hair still on, and dangling from the rearview mirror was a pair of little bitty cowboy boots made out of tooled leather.

"Cool," I breathed.

"Humph," Biggie said. "Somebody's got more money than taste."

"When I grow up, I'm going to get me a car like that," I said.

"Step lively," Biggie said. "We're most likely too late to get a table already."

Mr. Clovis Threadgill came riding his lawn mower around a black Suburban parked in front of the café. He had painted a sign on an old board and mounted it on the back of his mower. It read: "Birdsongs Are Palooters!!!"

Biggie stepped right in front of him so he had to stop. "Clovis, what in the blue-eyed world do you think you're doing?"

The old man drew his toy gun like he always does. He thinks he's an old-time cowboy from the movies. "Step aside, you sidewinders," he said. "I'm protestin'."

Biggie grinned. "Okay, honey, but stay out of the way, or Paul and Silas might have to drive you home in his police car."

"Biggie," I said as she pushed open the blue door, "I'm about half scared of that old man."

"I've known old Clovis all my life. He's a few bricks shy of a load, but he's harmless."

The café was packed. I guess everybody in Job's Crossing and some from out of town must have been there.

7

"Biggeee!" someone called. "Over here! We saved ya'll a seat."

We squeezed through the crowd to a table in the corner where Miss Mattie Thripp and her husband, Norman, were sitting with Miss Lonie Fulkerson and Butch.

"Put your purse in that extra chair," Miss Mattie said. "We're saving it for Paul and Silas—if he ever gets here, that is. He had to go work a wreck out on Farm Road Ninety-seven. One of those nasty old chicken trucks ran off the bridge, and all the chickens escaped."

"Hmmm," Biggie said, gazing around at the crowd, "I wonder where Firman is. It's unlike him not to be right in the middle of things."

Just then, Fairy Lee Watkins came over to our table, carrying a stack of blue menus printed all over with yellow baby chicks. "Ya'll mind sharing a menu?" she asked. "I declare, you wouldn't think these things would be so heavy, but they are. They got one hundred and one different choices for chicken in them."

"How are you folks going to prepare that many dishes?" Mr. Thripp asked. "It's all we can manage to offer six entrees down at the tearoom."

"Oh, Mr. Firman's got um all prepared and froze," Fairy Lee said. "He's got two of his Mexicans back in the kitchen. They just pop um in the microwave."

"Well, I sure wouldn't tell it," Miss Mattie said under her breath.

Butch took his teaspoon and fished something out of his water glass, then shook it off on the floor. "Ooh," he said, "do you have chicken divan? I had that once over in Shreveport. It was heavenly."

"You'll have to look on the menu, Mr. Butch," Fairy Lee said. "I gotta go now. I'll be back after ya'll's orders soon as I can."

"Here comes Ben Birdsong," Biggie said. "I've got a bone to pick with him.

"You mean a chicken bone," Miss Mattie giggled, smearing butter on a soda cracker.

"How you folks—well—what I mean to say is, how ya'll doing? Is the waitress, er, Fairy Lee taking care of you?"

"The poor thing ith juth running her little legth off," Miss Lonie said. "Why in the world didn't you hire extra help?"

Miss Lonie talks funny on account of being born tongue-tied, which is better than being born with two tongues like a man I saw at the State Fair of Texas. He couldn't even close his mouth all the way and had to be fed by a tube through his nose. I could have watched him eat, but they wanted a dollar more for it, and Biggie said I could see that any time I wanted. All I had to do was go with her to visit Aunt Bill Goolsby over at the rest home.

Mr. Ben looked down at the floor. "Well, uh—"

"Never mind that, Ben," Biggie said. "What I want to know is, what do you plan to do about those feathers you've dumped all over Job's Crossing. If we have a rain, the whole town's going to stink like a henhouse."

"Well, um," Mr. Ben said, "we've ordered a professional clean-up crew from Dallas. They said, well, I mean, they promised to come Monday to get started. I, um . . ."

"Okay, honey." Biggie put him out of his misery. "Send Fairy Lee over here. We're ready to order."

"What's the matter with that man?" Miss Mattie asked.

"He can't string three words together without tripping on his tongue."

"He's always been that way," Biggie said. "Firman does all the talking. Ben's a whiz with numbers, though. Truth to tell, it's probably because of Ben they've made such a success of Fresh-as-a-Daisy."

"Thath right," Miss Lonie said. "Firmanth alwayth gotten by on his lookth."

"Looks?" Mr. Thripp said. "Why, Firman Birdsong must weigh three hundred pounds or more."

"You didn't know him when he was young," Miss Mattie told him. "Firman used to be real handsome. Every girl in town was after him. Isn't that right, Biggie?"

Biggie nodded.

"Look, Biggie," I said, pointing at the door. "Those must be the people that own that car we saw."

The couple were both dressed western. Real western. And they were old, at least Biggie's age. The woman wore a skirt and a vest with fringe just like Dale Evans used to wear in those old Roy Rogers shows they still show on cable, and she had a cowgirl hat hanging around her neck on a string. Her hair was yellow, and she wore it in little ringlets around her face. The man had on a western suit, orange and white just like his car, with a starched white shirt and a black bolo tie with a big turquoise rock holding it together. His hair was black and shiny and slicked back from his weather-beaten face. He was brown like an Indian.

The two took a seat at the counter.

I heard Biggie draw in a breath, and when I looked at her, she was white as a ghost. "What in the world . . ." she said.

"What, Biggie? What's the matter?"

Biggie shook her head. "It's nothing. Never mind. Oh, here comes Fairy Lee to take our orders."

The food was nothing special. I was picking at my fried chicken tenders when I heard someone holler back in the kitchen like they'd seen a snake. Fairy Lee's husband, Dub Watkins, got off his stool at the counter and went charging through the swinging doors that led to the back. I looked around to see if anyone else had noticed, but they were all eating chicken and chatting with each other.

I nudged Biggie. "Somebody hollered in the kitchen. Biggie, you better go see about it."

Biggie put down her drumstick and smiled at me. "You think your Biggie has to take care of everything, don't you? Probably somebody just burned themselves."

"Uh-uh," I said. "It wasn't that kind of holler, Biggie—and Dub, he heard it, too. You better go, Biggie. I'm tellin' you."

Just then, Dub came out of the kitchen carrying Fairy Lee, who was out cold. He laid her down in a booth and headed back toward the kitchen. Biggie followed him, and I followed her.

We found Dub standing at the rear of the kitchen next to the big butcher-block worktable. When he saw Biggie, he pointed to the floor.

"What?" Biggie asked. "Did Fairy Lee fall down in this mess of gravy spilt on the floor?"

Dub didn't answer, just squatted down and pointed under the big table. I saw he had a tattoo of a heart stuck with a bloody dagger on his forearm. Then I saw what he was pointing at.

11

Somebody was lying under the table, and that somebody was covered from head to toe with white flour gravy. It covered his head and his arms and feet, his clothes, everything but his mouth, which had a tomato stuck in it. The gravy was starting to dry and crack in places, and—this is the really weird part—someone had sprinkled parsley all over him, then stuck a whole bunch right on top of his big old belly. I thought of the way Willie Mae garnishes food with parsley when we have company. There was something red mixed with the gravy right near his hairline.

"Go and lock the kitchen doors," Biggie told Dub, "then call the police station and find out if Paul and Silas is back from working that wreck. You two stay over there until the police come," she said to the two cooks who were shaking in their chef's hats.

Biggie knelt down and put her fingers on the man's neck, then pulled them back. "Hand me a towel, J.R.," she said. "He's been dead a while. Let's see who this is . . ." She swiped his face. "Just as I suspected, it's Firman."

Paul and Silas Wooten is Biggie's cousin from Tennessee, only we didn't know him until last year when he came to town on his motorcycle and rescued me and my friend, Monica, from some vicious kidnappers. Now he's our police chief. It's a good thing, too, because before that, we had Butch for a chief, and while Butch is good at a lot of things, like decorating and flower arranging, he was a real sorry excuse for a cop.

We didn't have to wait more than fifteen minutes before Paul and Silas tapped on the back door of the kitchen. By then, the crowd in the restaurant had gotten wind something was up, mainly because Fairy Lee had woke up and started hollering again. They were pushing against the doors and trying to look through the little glass windows.

After taking a look at Firman, Paul and Silas went to the door and ordered everyone to go back to their tables and wait for further orders.

"Butch," he said, "I'm deputizing you as of now. I want you to take the names and addresses of everybody here while I find out if the cooks know anything. Can you handle it?"

"Right, Chiefy-baby," Butch said. "I'm your man."

"Don't call me that." Paul and Silas turned red. "After that, I want you to take Miss Fairy Lee down to Doc Hooper's office and get him to give her a little something to calm her down. Then send him right here so he can pronounce this gentleman officially dead."

Biggie found Mr. Ben and told him what had happened. "Is there somebody I can call?" she asked. "Your wife?"

"No'm. She's gone to Shreveport shopping. I reckon I'll just wait around 'til everybody leaves and then lock up and go home."

"Go, now," Biggie said. "Give me your keys. I'll have Paul and Silas lock up for you. You can pick up the keys at the police station tomorrow when you come down to give a statement."

Mr. Ben looked relieved. "Thanks, Miss Biggie. I'll just do that, then. I reckon I'm . . . uh, well . . ."

Biggie patted him on the shoulder. "I know. Upset. Run along, now."

.   .   .

It was past ten when we got home. Biggie and I sat at the kitchen table and told Willie Mae and Rosebud what had happened.

"You ain't had nothing to eat?" Willie Mae asked.

"No, ma'am," I said. "I'm starved, too."

Before you could say boo to a goose, Willie Mae had whipped up a mess of hot biscuits and fried up some sausage patties. She sliced a ripe tomato to go with it and scrambled some eggs.

"Biggie," I said, "who were those strangers that came in the café? You seemed like you knew them."

"We'll talk about that later," Biggie said. "Right now, I'm hungry enough to eat a turkey buzzard."

"You want some gravy?" asked Willie Mae as she set our plates in front of us.

I looked at Biggie, and Biggie looked at me.

"No'm," I said.

2

I've lived with Biggie since I was six. That's the year my daddy died, and Mama couldn't take care of me any longer on account of her being the nervous type. Mama said I'd be better off here in Job's Crossing even if I did have to live with a crazy old white woman and two colored people. She said if I stayed in Dallas, I might join a gang or something while she was at work. Personally, I'd rather live with Biggie than be in a gang any old day. How many gang members get to live with Willie Mae, who is a real live voodoo woman? Or Rosebud, who tells the best stories in the whole world? Or Biggie, who runs the whole town and solves mysteries to boot? I was a happy kid until Skinny and Jane Culpepper came to town. They just about ruined everything. It all started the next day after Mr. Firman Birdsong got himself shot and gravied up like a fricasseed chicken. I was out back helping Rosebud build an arbor for Biggie's climbing roses when I heard the doorbell ring.

"I'll get it," I yelled. But by the time I got there, Biggie was greeting the cowboy couple we'd seen at the café the night before.

I followed them into the living room. Biggie was being polite, but she looked cautious, like a little dog with a big bone.

"Sit over there on the sofa," she said to the couple. "J.R., this is your other grandmother, Jane Culpepper, and her husband, Skinny."

I must have looked like I'd swallowed a frog, because I sure felt that way.

"Close your mouth, J.R.," Biggie said.

The woman sank down on Biggie's flowered sofa and held out her arms to me. "Come on over here and give your granny a big hug. I ain't seen you since you were no bigger'n a tadpole."

The man walked over to the window and stood looking out, whistling through his teeth.

I looked at Biggie.

"Go on," she said, "hug your other grandmother. I expect she's come a long way to see you. Where are you living now, Janie Pearl?"

"Just Jane," the woman said, wrapping her spongy arms around me. "I go by Jane now. Where do we live? Well, darlin', ever since I married Skinny here, we've lived up in Montana on our big old dude ranch." She lowered her voice. "Skinny, he's richer than you and God put together. Owns half of Montana—I swear! You see our new car out there? It's a classic. Skinny bought it off a dealer in Austin . . . seen it and liked it . . . plunked down twenty thousand right then and there . . . just wrote out a check for it. Looky here at the diamonds he's bought me."

When she let go of me to show off her rings, I escaped and plopped down on the floor next to Biggie's chair.

The man called Skinny came away from the window and sat on the sofa beside his wife. When I snuck a peek at him, he crossed his eyes and stuck out his tongue at me, then grinned. I had to cover my mouth to keep from grinning back. Then the man commenced whistling through his teeth again and stared at Biggie's portrait of her ancestor, James Royce Wooten, who I'm named after.

"What brings you to Job's Crossing?" Biggie asked. "I know it's not to see J.R., because you haven't sent him so much as a birthday card since the day he was born."

The woman didn't say anything, just started digging in the tooled leather saddlebag she used for a purse. She came out with a crumpled letter and handed it to Biggie. Biggie took the letter, and as she read it, her hands began to shake.

"J.R.," she said, "go into the kitchen and tell Willie Mae to make some coffee and cut that applesauce cake she made for dinner. You stay and help."

I knew she was trying to get rid of me, but I didn't have any choice—I had to go. When I came back carrying the tray full of coffee and cake, Biggie had a look on her face like those two were crabgrass and she was a goat. I wouldn't have wanted to be them. Still, when she spoke, her voice was soft and sweet as Willie Mae's muskydine jelly.

"J.R., honey," she said. "Your grandmother has a letter from your mama. I think you'd better read it."

I took the letter and read:

To Whom It May Concern:

I, Wanda Jo Weatherford, of Dallas County, Texas, do hereby confer full custody and care of my son, James Royce Weatherford III, to my mother, Jane Culpepper, and her husband, M. D. "Skinny" Culpepper, until the said James Royce Weatherford III, reaches the age of eighteen years.

It was signed by my mother and someone called Notary Public.

I looked at the woman with her cowboy clothes and diamonds and dyed hair. Then I looked at Biggie.

"I ain't going," I said.

Then Biggie said something I'll never forget as long as I live. "You have to, J.R.," she said. "It's the law."

The man, Skinny, took his coffee cup and went out to the front porch. I scooted closer to Biggie and listened while the woman talked, hating her more with every word.

"You see, it's like this," she said, reaching for a second piece of cake. "Skinny had a daughter once. When the girl was still in her teens, about twelve years ago, some seven-sided SOB came through town and knocked her up and then rode off into the sunset. She never was right after that."

"Did she have the baby?" Biggie asked.

"Dropped the kid right on schedule," the woman said,

"then took her daddy's shotgun and blew out her brains." Jane dug into her saddlebag and pulled out a red compact and commenced powdering her nose. Next, she pulled out a lipstick. "You like this color?" she asked Biggie. "It's burnt orange for the Texas Longhorns. I got it in Austin in a drugstore near the university."

"So, what happened to the baby?" I asked, thinking it would be just about my age by now.

"All this talking's making me dryer'n a West Texas arroyo," she said. "You got any bourbon an' branch water?"

Biggie rang the little bell beside her chair. In a minute Willie Mae came out of the kitchen.

"I got cookies in the oven," she said.

"Just bring Mrs. Culpepper a glass of that dewberry brandy you made," Biggie said.

Willie Mae grinned. "Yes, ma'am."

When she came back, she was carrying a tray with a jelly glass full of brandy.

"Be careful," Biggie warned. "Willie Mae's brandy will take the fillings out of your teeth."

"Thanks for the warning." The woman drained the glass and set it down with a thump. "Now, about the kid. We raised the little feller. Skinny was more than fond of him—spoilt him rotten. Give him everything."

"Why didn't you bring him with you?" I asked.

Jane Culpepper looked at me kind of bleary-eyed. I thought she might be about to keel over from drinking Willie Mae's brandy too fast, but she suddenly sat up straight, and her old blue eyes turned harder than frozen ball bearings.

"We'd've had to dig him up to do it," she said. "He got

killed last winter riding a dern snowmobile Skinny just had to buy even though the kid was way too young for it." She turned and faced Biggie. "That's why we got to have this kid," she said. "Skinny's been worthless as a bucket of spit since it happened."

"Well," Biggie changed the subject, "now I've got you here, I might as well ask you a few questions about the murder that happened last night at the restaurant. J.R., go ask Mr. Culpepper to come inside."

I went to the front porch and found the man sitting on the swing holding Booger, who normally doesn't much like strangers. But now, he was letting Skinny scratch him under the neck and purring like a freight train. I don't know why I did it, but I grabbed Booger and threw him off the porch into Biggie's mock orange tree. He scrambled back to the porch rail and sat with his back to us, licking hard.

"Biggie wants you inside," I said, then ran around back to find Rosebud.

He was sitting at the kitchen table drinking coffee and eating Willie Mae's fresh peanut butter cookies. Willie Mae poured me a glass of cold milk and set it down, then rumpled my hair with her hand.

"You know, then?" I asked.

"Course," she said. I wasn't surprised, because Willie Mae knows everything on account of being a voodoo woman.

"What are we going to do, Willie Mae?" I said. "Biggie seems like she's just going to let them take me."

"You ain't goin'," Willie Mae said.

"Course not," Rosebud said, but he didn't sound so certain.

"Are you going to do voodoo, Willie Mae?" I asked.

"Maybe so; maybe not," she said. "But you ain't goin'. Now you two better git out there and finish up Miss Biggie's rose arbor."

Than night after supper, Biggie sent me to the attic to bring down the big box of Christmas ornaments.

"When can we put up the tree, Biggie?" I asked.

"The first Sunday in Advent like we always do. J.R., you know that."

"What if I'm not here? What if I'm already in Montana by Christmas?"

Biggie looked up from the string of lights she was untangling. "Come here," she said.

I went and stood beside her, and she put both arms around me. "J.R.," she said, "I'll fight a boxcar load of wildcats before I let anyone take you away from me. Don't you know that?"

"But that letter from Mama . . ." I said.

Just then, Rosebud came in carrying a big bowl of buttered popcorn. "Ranch life ain't so bad," he said. "I recollect the time I was cowboyin' for the Z-Bar-J up near Billings. We got to roundin' up strays and didn't realize the biggest blizzard of the season was bearin' down on us. . . ."

"You were a cowboy?" I asked.

"Sure was. I don't like to brag, doncha know, but old man Dolinsky, he owned the spread, he give me four brand-new fifty-dollar bills for bringin' down his favorite little dogie off that mountain in forty feet of snow."

"Uh-uh," I said.

"If I'm lyin', I'm dyin'," he said. "Looky here on my ear. You see that white spot? That there's where I got frost-bit that very night."

I looked but couldn't see any white spot.

"Must've gone away," Rosebud said. "Used to be big as a quarter. Miss Biggie, did them folks know anything about that murder?"

"Not much. They were together in their hotel room watching the news before they got dressed and came to the restaurant. They both swear they weren't out of each other's sight except to go to the bathroom." She scooped up a handful of popcorn and washed it down with coffee.

"So, could they have slipped to the back while nobody was lookin'?"

"It's possible, but they didn't arrive until after we did, and Firman had been dead for quite some time before that."

"How come you know that?" Rosebud asked.

"Because the gravy had already congealed and dried out in spots," Biggie said. "He must have been dead for at least an hour before Fairy Lee found him."

" 'Sides that," Rosebud said, "them folks didn't even know Mr. Firman."

Biggie stared at the fire for a long time. "Nobody's above suspicion," she said. "Good grief, look at the time. Hop off to bed, J.R., school's tomorrow."

I had a real hard time getting to sleep. I kept thinking about how awful it would be to have to go to Montana and live with those Culpeppers. He didn't seem so bad, but my other grandmother, she was a mean woman who didn't act like she cared one bit that a little boy got himself killed in a snowmobile wreck. Of course, I'd just have to run away and never come back to Job's Crossing. I'd start planning it first thing in the morning.

Just as I was about to doze off, I heard the door open and close real softly. I opened one eye and saw Biggie standing beside my bed. I didn't feel like talking, so I pretended to be asleep. She stood there a long time, then kissed me, tucked me in, and tiptoed out the door.

3

When I got home from school the next day, I found Paul and Silas and Butch sitting by the fire with Biggie and Rosebud. They were drinking spiced tea and talking about Mr. Birdsong.

"What did Doc find when he cleaned Firman up?" Biggie asked.

"Well, Cousin Biggie," Paul and Silas said, reaching for another piece of Willie Mae's applesauce cake, "Doc says a twenty-two slug pierced his brain at medium range. Not close enough for burning the skin, but close enough to go right through his skull."

"It might've been suicide," Butch said. "I heard down at the café that Fresh-as-a-Daisy's not doing near 'bout as good as the Birdsongs would have you believe. Maybe Firman was depressed and decided to end it all."

Rosebud slapped his knee and laughed out loud. "And then poured gravy over hisself and stuck a tomater in his mouth," he said. "Reckon how he got that parsley sprinkled all over him?"

"Oh," said Butch, "I didn't think about that. That was ugly. Whoever did that was a real mean person, that's all I've got to say. What kind of flowers do ya'll think would be nice for a casket spray? I was thinking white lilies with a few red carnations sprinkled here and about."

I thought about all that white gravy and the red tomato in his mouth and made a face.

"Cousin Biggie," Paul and Silas said, "would you mind taking a ride with me? I have something to show you that may well pertain to this case."

"Well, I can't go," Butch said. "I've got to fly back to the shop before that Meredith Michelle Muckleroy takes a notion to go off following some boy—that girl is just boy crazy."

"I promised Willie Mae I'd peel the sweet potatoes for supper," Rosebud said. "You mind if I stay here, Miss Biggie?"

"Nope," Biggie said. "Paul and Silas can drive us in the police car."

I rode in back behind the cage where the prisoners ride.

"Pee-yew," I said.

"Sorry, cousin," Paul and Silas said. "I had to transport Cooter McNutt from the Dumpster behind the Eazee Freeze to jail. It doesn't take a minute for Cooter to foul up a place."

"What had he done?" I asked.

"Made a mess. He'd scattered garbage all over the parking lot looking for a pair of boots he'd heard Roy Lee Peoples had thrown out."

"Did he find the boots?" I asked.

"J.R.," Biggie said, "you're nosier than Lonie Fulkerson."

"Yes'm."

Paul and Silas drove out Karnes Chapel Road that goes out past the lakes and turned down a gravel road just past the Wooten Creek bridge. A mailbox beside the road read "Threadgill." I kind of wished I'd stayed home with Willie Mae and Rosebud.

We pulled into the driveway of a neat little white farmhouse with a John Deere riding lawn mower parked in front. Paul and Silas honked the horn.

Pretty soon, out came Mr. Threadgill, strapping on his holster with its toy gun. Once he got it on, he stood spraddle-legged in front of his door and drew down on us.

"Take one more step and you're all buzzard bait!" he hollered.

Paul and Silas held up his hand. "Now, Clovis, I just want you to show Miss Biggie how your creek's been polluted. Remember, you told me about that?"

The old man holstered his pistol. "Okay, long as that's all you want. Just hold your horses while I git my boots on."

He disappeared into his house and came back out wearing boots and a black cowboy hat with a white turkey feather stuck in the band. He slung his leg over the lawn mower like it was a horse. "Foller me!" he yelled.

"We might just as well walk, Cousin Biggie," Paul and

Silas said. "It's only a quarter mile or so. See that line of trees over there? Well, that's the creek. It's also Mr. Threadgill's property line. Birdsongs own the adjoining land."

I could hear the old man yodeling as he bumped across the pasture. Suddenly he stopped and pointed.

"What's that smell?" Biggie asked as we got closer to the trees. "Pee-yew! It smells like rotten eggs."

"Yeah," I said to Paul and Silas. "That's worse than your police car."

Biggie trotted up ahead of us until she was standing beside Mr. Threadgill at the creek bank. "Lordy mercy," she said. "It *is* rotten eggs!"

Sure enough, right across the barbwire fence that surrounded Mr. Threadgill's place was a draw, and that draw was filled up with a mountain of eggs, broken and rotting and oozing right into Mr. Threadgill's creek. I saw a nice perch floating belly-up in the water.

"It's ugly, Biggie," I said. "Why do you reckon they'd want to do that?"

"I don't know, honey," Biggie said, "but I aim to find out. Now, don't you worry, Clovis. We'll see that this is stopped. Yessiree-bob!"

"I don't need no help from no town tenderfoots, not as long as I got my shootin' iron," he said. "I done got one of them Birdbrains. Just give me time, I'll git t'other."

On the way back to town, we met those Culpeppers in their fancy car. Old Jane (I wouldn't call her Granny if she tortured me with red-hot needles) must've seen me because she reached across Skinny and mashed the horn. It played "The Eyes of Texas Are Upon You" so loud I about jumped out of my skin. I wouldn't look at them, though.

When we got home, Willie Mae had supper on the table. Red beans, cornbread, grits cooked with green chilies, ham, and red-eye gravy.

"Yum," Biggie said. "I could eat half a sow."

"Me, too!" I said, sliding into a chair and sniffing the steam coming off the ham. "That smells good."

"Best you ever laid a lip over," Rosebud said.

"Git up from there and go wash your hands," Willie Mae said.

"Biggie," I said later, sopping up the last of my gravy with my fourth biscuit, "I reckon your case is solved. Mr. Threadgill said he did it. How come Paul and Silas didn't arrest him right then?"

"J.R., what are you talking about?" Biggie said. "Willie Mae, would you put just a little more grits on my plate?"

"I don't know why you don't git fat," Willie Mae said, spooning more grits on Biggie's plate.

"Biggie, weren't you listening? That old man said he killed Mr. Birdsong."

"I know he said it, J.R., but Clovis hasn't got brains enough to fill an acorn shell. Most of the time, he doesn't know come here from sic 'em."

"Sounds to me like the old feller's got a problem with them eggs, though," Rosebud said.

Willie Mae went into the kitchen and came back out carrying a sweet potato pie in one hand and a bowl of whipped cream in the other.

"Who wants pie?"

"Me," I said, "plenty of whipped cream."

Biggie nodded to Willie Mae and turned back to Rosebud. "You're right," she said. "Those Birdsongs must have gotten just a little too big for their britches. Imagine, thinking they could run over their neighbors like that. Oh, well, I plan to question Ben as soon as the funeral's over. I'll tell him he can't go dumping his waste just anywhere he pleases. If he argues, I'll simply remind him of my cousin, H. Ross Weatherford, who serves on the water board in Austin." She held out her plate for more pie. "I'm sure he'll understand."

"When is they gonna funeralize him, Miss Biggie?" Willie Mae wanted to know.

"I heard it was Wednesday," I said.

"Is your name Biggie?" Willie Mae asked.

"No'm."

"Well—"

"I believe it is Wednesday," Biggie said. "Our state senator is coming here to deliver the eulogy. As you know, Firman was quite active in Austin. More than likely, there'll be more politicians here than ticks on a coonhound."

"You goin', Miss Biggie?" Willie Mae asked. "Because, if you are, I gotta get your black dress cleaned. You ruint that blue one messin' around that murder."

"I don't think I'll go, honey," Biggie said. "I'm thinking that might be a good day to inspect the crime scene while everyone else is at the funeral." She popped the last bite of pie in her mouth and drained her coffee cup. "J.R.," she said, "I want you to help Willie Mae with the dishes, then go upstairs and get your homework. I'll be in to say good night."

While I was drying the dishes I said, "Willie Mae, have you figured out a way to keep me from having to go to Montana?"

"What you talkin' about, boy?" She scowled at me.

"You know. You said I didn't have to go."

"You git you another dryin' rag. That thing's soppin' wet."

"Willie Mae!"

"I said you ain't goin', and you ain't. Now git upstairs and git your lessons!"

I hadn't thought too much about the Culpeppers all day, but now that I was faced with going to sleep in the dark again, the worry started coming back.

When Biggie came to tuck me in, I had to force back the tears.

"What's wrong, J.R.?" Biggie asked.

"Nothin'."

Just then, Booger jumped into my lap. I buried my face in his fur.

"Is it those Culpeppers?"

I don't know why, but I got real mad. "Of course it is, Biggie." Now I couldn't keep the tears from running down my face. "I'm going to have to live with those people, and nobody cares. Ya'll just go about your business like nothing bad's about to happen."

Biggie put her arms around me and pulled me to her. "J.R., have I ever in your whole life let you down?"

"No'm."

"Then you just have to believe I won't do it this time, honey. Now, they can't leave town until we get this murder solved, and that may not be until after the new year. I want you to have a good time and look forward to Christmas just like every other year. I'll never let anyone take you away from me!"

30

I looked up at Biggie and saw tears in her eyes and wondered if, for the first time, we had come up against something even she couldn't control.

That night I dreamed I was an Indian, and about a million cowboys were coming after me to take my scalp.

4

Wednesday was a teacher workday, so I got to stay home from school. When I came down for breakfast, Biggie and Willie Mae had commenced baking. Willie Mae was rolling piecrusts on the table while Biggie stirred something on the stove that smelled like spices and maple sugar.

"Ummm. Can I have some?" I said.

"Do these pies look like they ready?" Willie Mae asked.

"No'm."

"Then git you some cereal and go in the den and eat it," she said.

"They're for the Christmas bazaar, J.R.," Biggie said. "You'll have to buy one if you expect to get a bite of these pies." Biggie grinned. She knows how much I hate to take money out of my bank. I've got $83.56 in there, and I'm saving for something really important.

I poured me a bowl of cereal and went into the den and turned on the TV to one of those talk shows. Some girl was beating another girl over the head with her purse on account of the first girl was messing with the other girl's boyfriend, who happened to be her own stepdad. I turned the TV off and went to sit on the front porch. Rosebud was weeding Biggie's chrysanthemums. He didn't look up at me.

"Whatcha doin'?" I said, just to make conversation.

Rosebud still didn't look up. "What do it look like I'm doin'?"

"Well, weeding. But here's the thing. I'm off from school today."

"So?" Rosebud didn't take his eyes off the crabgrass he was digging up.

"So? Rosebud, what do you mean, 'so'? What can we do on my day off?"

Rosebud squatted back on his heels and wiped his face with a blue bandanna. "You think I got nothin' to do but play with you? Shoot, them womens give me a list of jobs that's long as my arm. I prob'ly won't git through 'til after Christmas."

"Christmas!" I said. "Hey, Rosebud, I just now remembered. They're putting up the Christmas decorations around the square today. Chief Frobisher's gonna bring the fire truck down so they can use the ladders to climb on."

Rosebud pushed his old straw hat back and scratched his head. "I believe you're right," he said. "They might need our help."

"Well, come on!" I said.

When we got to the square, we found the street blocked off with yellow tape so nobody could drive through. The fire truck was parked by the curb, and Mr. Thripp was standing on top of the big ladder hanging tinsel. Chief Frobisher was halfway up handing him stuff. The daughters and Butch were on the ground giving out advice. It looked awful. The swags were uneven, some hanging down almost as low as Rosebud's head.

"Where is Biggie?" Mrs. Muckleroy wanted to know. "We were supposed to meet here at nine."

"Baking pies with Willie Mae," I said.

"Well, I never," said Mrs. Muckleroy. "And her chapter president, too."

"I reckon she forgot," I said.

"Biggie never forgets," Mrs. Vestal Chapman said. "I declare, that woman's got a mind like a brand-new pipe organ. I reckon she just didn't want to come."

"She's makin' pies for the bazaar," I said.

"I remember now," said Miss Julia Lockhart, who writes a column for the paper. "Biggie's on the bazaar committee, not the decorating committee."

Mrs. Muckleroy looked disappointed. She's all the time trying to catch Biggie doing something wrong.

Butch was standing in the street surrounded by a big pile of silver and red tinsel with glittery silver stars tied on it. "Ya'll get that tighter, you hear?" he called. "First rain we get, that'll drag the ground."

I thought I heard Mr. Thripp say something not very nice, but I wasn't sure. Then he dropped a whole line of tinsel, and it fell on Mrs. Muckleroy's head.

"Oh, my gracious," Butch said, "at this rate, we ain't

34

never going to get through. And I've got to get the flowers out to Mr. Birdsong's funeral."

"Let me up there," Rosebud said, so Mr. Thripp came down and Rosebud took his place.

I stayed on the ground and helped the ladies and Butch make red bows to hang on the parking meters. Butch had cut little Jesuses, Marys, and Josephs out of cardboard to go in the middle of each bow. He'd painted them with poster paint, then sprinkled glitter over the paint. "I think it's so much nicer to remember the *real* meaning of Christmas," he said. "Don't ya'll? This year, all my decorations are going to have a religious theme."

Miss Lonie held up a cutout of Mary wearing a red robe. "I thought the Virgin alwayth wore blue," she said.

"Bor-ring," Butch said.

Out of the corner of my eye, I saw something big and black speeding toward the square from the direction of our house. It was Biggie driving her car, and she didn't even slow down at the yellow tape barricade, just busted on through and came to a stop next to the fire truck.

"Uh-oh," Rosebud said.

Biggie got out of the car and stood with her hands on her hips, looking around at the tinsel and bows all over the sidewalk, then up the ladder at Rosebud.

"Well," she said, "looks like you're needed here more than at home, Rosebud. But from the looks of things, you won't be finished until Christmas has come and gone. Why are you all just standing around?" she said to the crowd that had gathered to watch. "Let's all pitch in."

Before long, Biggie was bossing everybody around, and by noon the square looked downright Christmasy.

"Come on, you two," Biggie said, getting back in her car. "Willie Mae's got chicken spaghetti for lunch."

"Biggie," Miss Julia said, "will we see you at the funeral?"

"Nope," Biggie said, rolling up her car window. "I've got other plans."

Willie Mae had cooked a casserole of chicken spaghetti with lots of cheese melted on top. She also had field peas, cornbread, bread and butter pickles, and Jell-O salad. The iced tea was sweetened just the way I like and had slices of lime stuck between the ice cubes.

"Willie Mae," Biggie said after we'd all sat down to eat, "will you be needing Rosebud this afternoon?"

Rosebud shook his head. "I ain't nothing but an appliance around here. Might just as well be the washin' machine."

Willie Mae ignored him. "I was gonna have him vacuum down the drapes in the front room," she said, "but he can do that Saturday, I reckon."

"Good." Biggie piled peas on top of a big slab of cornbread. "I need him to drive J.R. and me down to the Fresh-as-a-Daisy Restaurant. I want to question Fairy Lee. Do we have any of that chowchow left?"

Willie Mae reached into the fridge and handed Biggie a jar of chowchow. Biggie spooned a big glob on top of her peas and cornbread.

"Biggie," I said, "do I have to go? I wanted to work on my model."

"Yep," she said, talking with her mouth full, which she will never let me do, "I need your eyes and ears—Rosebud's too."

. . .

The restaurant was closed on account of Mr. Birdsong's funeral, but Fairy Lee had agreed to meet Biggie there at two because she said she just couldn't bear to watch them put poor Mr. Birdsong in the ground. She was scrubbing the counter with Lysol even though everything in the place was brand-new.

"I cain't help it," she said. "I just got to get the smell of death out of here. Mr. Firman would want it. Ya'll want some coffee?"

"Sure, honey," Biggie said, "and then I want you to tell me everything that happened on the night of the murder. Start with when you got to work."

"Lemme see," Fairy Lee said, "I reckon I must've got here near a quarter to five. Dub drove to my house right after he got off his run. He had to drive a load of turkeys over to Mount Particular." She spit on her rag and scrubbed an invisible spot off the coffeemaker. "Course I told him not to even bother to come get me unless he washed up and put on a clean shirt, doncha know. So I suppose it musta been four-thirty when he picked me up."

"Were you the first to arrive?" Biggie asked.

"Yes'm, I reckon. Mr. Ben came along soon after, though, bringing them Mesican chefs. J.R., you want a Coke?"

"I'll take a Big Red," I said.

"What did you do when you got here?" Biggie asked.

"Oh, the usual stuff, you know. Since it was grand opening, we was expecting a crowd at six. That's when the doors was to open."

Fairy Lee patted her hair, which was real long and done

up in rolls and curls on top of her head. Fairy Lee belongs to one of those churches that don't let the women cut their hair. She didn't have on any makeup, either, but she was pretty anyway.

"What kind of 'usual stuff'?" Rosebud asked.

"Oh, like makin' the tea and coffee, settin' out the napkins and glasses and cups. Stuff like that."

"I reckon you had to go in the kitchen, huh?" Rosebud said.

"Not all that much," Fairy Lee said. "See, we keep most of the serving stuff out front here. It's more, you know, convenient that way. And like, somebody comes in, just wants coffee or a cold drink, I got everything I need right here behind the—"

"Right," Biggie said. "So you didn't go back to the kitchen at all?"

Fairy Lee was standing behind the counter leaning on her elbows; we sat on stools. She turned and reached for the coffeepot. "More?" she asked.

"I'll have just a tad," Biggie said. "Now, did you have to go to the kitchen?"

"Only once. I thought I heard a noise comin' from back there, like maybe Mr. Ben had left the teakettle on. That Mr. Ben sure likes his tea. Anyway, when I got there, I saw someone had spilled gravy—oh, my stars!"

"It's okay, honey," Biggie said. "So, what did you do?"

"Praise God," Fairy Lee said, "poor Mr. Firman must've been under that table—oh, lordy, and I didn't even see him."

"What did you do?" Biggie asked again.

Fairy Lee smoothed her apron. "Well, I just swiped up

that gravy the best I could. Then I heard the first customers come in, and after that, I was busier than a grasshopper in a fire ant bed. I figured them chefs would clean up the mess."

Biggie set down her coffee cup. "Just one more question, honey. How did you get along with the Birdsong brothers?"

"Just fine," Fairy Lee said real fast. "That is, well, I guess I got along better with Mr. Firman. He was real nice to me—once he even took me over to one of them gamblin' boats at Bossier City. He let me play the slots all day long. Every time I'd run out of quarters, here he'd come with another cupful."

"What would Brother Bob down at your church think of that?" Biggie asked.

Fairy Lee looked scared. "He don't know. Miss Biggie, you ain't gonna tell him, are you?"

"Not on your life," Biggie said. "By the way, how's your mama?"

"Fine, just fine. She's just bought her a new living room suite—three pieces—and a great huge entertainment center to put the TV on. You oughta go over and see it, Miss Biggie."

"I might just do that. Now, honey, you know not to leave town, don't you?"

"Where'd I go, Miss Biggie?"

After that, Biggie went in to inspect the kitchen, but Fairy Lee had scrubbed all the clues away with Lysol. Just as we were starting out the door, Rosebud stopped and walked over to the back window.

"Me, oh my," he said, "would you looky here." He was pointing to a tiny round hole in the brand-new window glass.

That night, Biggie said, "Sunday's the first day of Advent, J.R. Know what that means?"

"The Christmas tree! Can we go out to the farm to cut one on Saturday? I want a big old cedar this year."

"The biggest one we can find," Biggie said. "Rosebud, you'd better sharpen your ax."

I wondered what had come over Biggie. Usually, she wants some little old dinky thing she can set on the table in the parlor.

"What you plannin' for tomorrow, Miss Biggie?" Rosebud asked.

"A visit to the Fresh-as-a-Daisy chicken plant," Biggie said. "I want to see what Ben has to say about Firman's murder."

Willie Mae looked up from the pecans she was shelling. "While you're out there, you just as well reserve a turkey for Christmas dinner," she said. "I wants one that'll dress out at eighteen pounds or more. Tell Mr. Ben to put him in a pen and start right in feedin' him corn."

When I went to bed, I fell asleep right off. I even forgot to worry about those Culpeppers. I guess that was a mistake, though, because they sure managed to mess up my Christmas that year.

5

"Miss Biggie," Mr. Ben Birdsong said, "we've added a—well, it's what you might call a new feature to our operation." He wiped sweat off his head with a blue bandanna even though the wind was blowing colder than a frosted frog, and I was shivering in my Dallas Cowboys jacket. Me and Biggie had gone out to Fresh-as-a-Daisy to question Mr. Ben and pick out a turkey for Christmas dinner.

"You don't say." Biggie looked toward the big corrugated tin building where they keep the turkeys all jammed together on wire shelves. The reason they do that is so that when the turkeys poop, it falls down in drawers below to be scooped up and used to make fertilizer. I know all about it because when I was in third grade, our teacher took us on a tour of the plant. Mr. Firman was our guide, and he told us they use everything on the turkey but the gobble and the beak. He said he had a deal in the works then to sell the beaks to a designer in Paris, France, to be used in making fashion jewelry.

"Yes, ma'am," Mr. Ben said to Biggie, "we're offering our customers whatcha call free-range birds, doncha know."

"No, I don't know, Ben," Biggie said. "What in this ever-loving world is a free-range bird?"

"All natural. That's what folks want nowadays. See, we have this big, well, pen sort of thing, and the birds just walk around on the ground. Free, so to speak. We don't give them growth hormones or nothing. Just let them grow normally. Naturally, they cost more to raise that way, so we have to charge more for them." Mr. Ben let out a big sigh like it had worn him out to say so much. "Miss Biggie, do you reckon Willie Mae would want one of those birds?"

"Ben, honey, I grew up with yard birds. I thought it was progress when we started caging poultry and feeding them grain instead of letting them scratch around on the ground eating grubs and rocks and each other's droppings. Now, why in this world would I want to pay more to go backward?" She headed toward the turkey building. Me and Mr. Ben followed.

It felt good inside. Big fans were blowing warm air down from the ceiling. The turkeys were all gobbling softly to each other and pecking at their turkey food—all but one, that is. He towered over all the others and, the minute we walked in, let out a gobble that would wake up everybody in Wooten Creek cemetery. He glared and shook his wattles at Biggie.

"I'll take that one," Biggie said.

On the way back to Mr. Ben's office, Biggie explained to

him how Willie Mae wanted the turkey put in a coop and fed nothing but corn until Christmas.

Mr. Ben took a seat in his squeaky swivel chair while me and Biggie sat on a big comfortable leather couch. The office, on the fourth floor of the main building, was pretty spiffy for a chicken man, I thought. The carpet was soft as a calf's ear and had designs of red roosters on a real light-yellow background. A great huge window gave a view of the processing plant and barns as well as the hills and trees beyond. One wall was covered with framed photographs. There were mountains and rivers, the desert, and one real pretty one of the sun setting over the ocean. Mr. Ben saw me looking at the pictures.

"Firman took every one of them," he said. "Right nice for an amateur, doncha think?"

Biggie got up and walked over to the picture wall. "I didn't know Firman had been to all those places," she said.

"Oh, yes'm," Mr. Ben said. " 'Bout fifteen years ago, I reckon it was. Firman had him one of them midlife crisises you hear so much about. He always was the restless type. He hit the road and never came back for close to two years. Said he had to 'find himself,' whatever that means."

"What do you know," Biggie said. "And did he?"

"What?" Mr. Ben asked.

"What you just said, find himself."

Mr. Ben took off his shoe and scratched his foot. "Never did ask him. Still and all, he seemed like he, you know, settled down after that. After Firman came back, that's when Fresh-as-a-Daisy just, what you might say, took off."

Mr. Ben reached across his desk and took the lid off a

candy dish shaped like a hen on a nest. It was filled with candy corn. He passed it to Biggie, who shook her head, then to me. I took two pieces and popped them in my mouth. Willie Mae says if you eat candy corn, you'll have to go to the dentist and get false teeth before you're forty on account of it's just like eating pure sugar. I don't care. Biggie's got false teeth, and it sure doesn't slow her down any. I'll bet she can put away more ribs and corn on the cob than a whole roomful of dentists.

Biggie handed the dish back to Mr. Ben. "Hmm," she said, "now that you mention it, I do seem to recall Firman being wild as a peach-orchard boar in his younger days."

"Yes'm, you might say that." He smiled like he was remembering some secret. "That brother of mine would go bear hunting with a switch. And fight? That boy would pa-a-a-ay to fight. Why, if I'd've done half what Firman done, Papa would've had my hide."

"Your daddy was a preacher, wasn't he?"

"Yes'm. Hard-shell Baptist. Papa could see evil in the crotch of a tree."

"You were the oldest?"

"Yes'm."

"And you were the good son, I'll bet."

Mr. Ben looked out the window at the hills and trees. He spoke so low I had to strain to hear. "Yes'm. Dependable and dull, that was me. Firman, though, he wasn't scared of nobody—Papa included. He'd chuck rocks at Papa's mule, Gus, to see how high he'd kick. And once he tied two of Mama's kittens' tails together and slung them over the clothesline so he could watch them fight. They dern near clawed each other to death before I got them down. And another time, when Papa was havin' a foot washin' at the church, Firman took everybody's shoes and pitched them in the creek. Mama and Papa didn't do nothing. Seemed like they thought everything he done was cute."

"That must have been hard on you," Biggie said.

Mr. Ben shook his head and smiled. "No, ma'am." He looked down at his hands twisting his handkerchief into a ball. "That Firman, he could charm the air out of your tires—if you let him."

Biggie looked at her watch. "Look at the time," she said. "J.R., we've got to go." She made like she was about to get up, then sat back down again. "By the way, Ben, what time did you arrive at the café the night Firman was shot?"

Mr. Ben pulled a big black book from his desk drawer and opened it. "I can tell you exactly. I write down everything in this book. Leave nothing to chance, that's my motto. Let's see now, meeting at three . . . worked on the books until five-oh-two . . . made a few calls, then left for the day. That would put me at the café at exactly five-thirteen." He closed the book with a snap.

"Did you see Firman when you got there?" Biggie asked.

"Well, um, that was odd," Mr. Ben said. "He was supposed to meet me to discuss something important. But when I got there, he wasn't . . . I mean, I didn't know. . . ." He blew his nose with a loud honk.

"Mind telling me what you had to discuss?" Biggie asked.

"It was a, um, personnel matter. I hope you won't let

45

this get around." Mr. Ben patted his brow with his hankie. "That Dub's a rough character. I wouldn't want him to get wind of anything—"

"It was about Dub?"

"Yes'm, it was. You see, Firman had got all lathered up and wanted to fire Dub. Well, I told him not to be hasty. There's lots of things to be considered—like a big hike in our unemployment taxes, for one. You have to be real careful before you fire a feller, or he'll just go out and file for unemployment and your taxes can go sky . . ."

"Why did Firman want to fire him?" Biggie wanted to know.

"On account of Fairy Lee, you know, our waitress. She claimed old Dub was stalking her. Well, Firman, you know, couldn't ever resist a pretty face. I told him, I said, Firman, this ain't any of our business. That's when my brother dropped a clod in the churn."

"How's that?"

"Said he wanted to marry her! I like to died! Him almost fifty years old and her barely out of her teens and married, to boot."

"Didn't Fairy Lee divorce Dub?"

"Tried to. At least that's what she was tellin' my brother. And I reckon she wouldn't lie, being a Holy Roller and all, but she dropped it, the divorce, I mean, on account of old Dub kept driving by her house and calling her up on the phone, then hanging up. She claims he threatened that if she went through with it, he'd kill her dead." Mr. Ben opened his desk drawer and pulled out a pack of Juicy Fruit. "Gum?" he said. "All this talking's making me dry as a wooden leg."

I took a piece, but Biggie shook her head.

"So Firman wasn't around when you got to the café?" Biggie asked.

"I never saw him," Mr. Ben said. "I looked around some, but by six o'clock the customers had started to arrive. I just figured we'd talk about Dub the next day." Mr. Ben blew his nose again. "Course, I never thought there wasn't going to be any next day. Miss Biggie, have you questioned Dub yet?"

"Nope. But don't you worry, honey, I will." Biggie stood up. "Come on, J.R. We'd best be getting out of Ben's way. I'm sure he's got lots of work to do, what with Firman gone and all."

Mr. Ben followed us out to the car. "I reckon there's one other thing I ought to tell you," he said.

"Shoot," Biggie said.

"It may not mean anything, but when I walked into the café, I heard Dub and Fairy Lee having one heck of a fight. He was telling her he'd better not ever see her around that fat little chicken plucker (meaning, of course, my brother) or he'd haul off and kick her butt up between her shoulder blades. Excuse my French, Miss Biggie, but that's what he said."

"It's okay," Biggie said. "Now, honey, I want you to promise to get in touch with me if you think of anything else. Okay?"

Mr. Ben said he would and helped Biggie into the car. As we drove away, Biggie ran smack into a sign that said, FRESH-AS-A-DAISY CHICKEN MANURE—STRAIGHT AHEAD. She rolled down the window and called to Mr. Ben to send her the bill and she'd pay to have it fixed.

We were almost to town when I thought of something. "I've got it, Biggie," I said. "I betcha I know who shot Mr. Firman. It was—"

"Oh, looky there," Biggie said, "isn't that Norman and Mattie's car?"

"Where?"

"Parked beside the road ahead. See, the hood's up."

I looked. "Yep, and that looks like Mr. Thripp with his head under there. Know what, Biggie? I bet they've got car trouble. You better stop."

Biggie pulled up beside the Thripps' car and honked her horn real loud. She probably shouldn't have done that, because Mr. Thripp jumped and his arm hit the thing that holds the hood up, which caused the hood to come crashing down on his head.

Miss Mattie was picking persimmons in a field beside the road. When she heard Biggie's horn, she came back, stepping high over the bull nettles.

Biggie got out of the car, and I ran to hold the barbwire up so Miss Mattie could crawl through the fence.

"Look what I found," she said, showing us what was in the paper sack she was holding. "Good, ripe persimmons. I know they're good because we had that nice frost night before last."

"They are nice," Biggie said, looking into Miss Mattie's sack. "What are you going to do with them?"

"Make persimmon bread," Miss Mattie said. "You make it just like banana bread only you use persimmons instead of bananas."

"Do you put pecans in yours?" Biggie asked. "Willie Mae always uses pecans."

"Urrrgh!" Mr. Thripp said from under the car hood.

"I use walnuts," Miss Mattie said. "I think they're crunchier than pecans."

"Can I have one?" I asked.

"Help!" Mr. Thripp said, kicking the fender. "Oh, ouch!"

"Sure," Miss Mattie said, "take two. I've got more than I need here. They don't last, you know," she said to Biggie.

"Looks like you've got car trouble," Biggie said.

Miss Mattie looked toward the car for the first time. "It's the battery, I think. Norman's just no good with mechanical things. Would you just look. He's gone and let the hood fall on him. By the way, what are you two doing out this way?"

"Visiting with Ben Birdsong about the murder," Biggie said, "and I must say, he doesn't seem very broken up about the whole thing."

"Well," Miss Mattie said, "maybe he did it. Who else would have more to gain?"

"I don't think so," Biggie said. "Ben knows Firman was the creative force behind the business. Ben's nothing but a bean counter, if you know what I mean."

"HELP!" Mr. Thripp said.

"Norman seems to be getting impatient," Biggie said. "You can ride back to town with us, then get Aubrey Dunbar to come out and tow your car in. J.R, go over and help Mr. Thripp out from under that hood."

That night after supper, Willie Mae said we could make popcorn balls to hang on the Christmas tree. She spread a piece of plastic over the kitchen table, and we all sat around molding the popcorn and sticky syrup into balls.

Rosebud held up one for us to see. "How 'bout this'un? I made old Santy Claus. See here, I got green gumdrops for eyes and a red one for his nose."

"That don't look like Santa Claus," I said. "It looks like Mr. Firman all covered with gravy and parsley with a tomato in his mouth. Yuck!"

"We don't want no Santy Clauses," Willie Mae said. "Just balls I can wrap in cellophane papers for hanging."

"That reminds me," Biggie said. "J.R., what did you mean when you said you knew who did the murder?"

"That Dub," I said. "Remember, Biggie? Fairy Lee said Mr. Firman had taken her to Bossier to play the slot machines. I don't reckon old Dub would like that very much. Do you? So he probably took a notion to shoot Mr. Firman in the head. That's what I think."

"I'd already thought of that," Biggie said. "I plan to question him first thing tomorrow. But this time I think Paul and Silas had better go along in case there's trouble."

As it turned out, I'm sure glad he did.

6

Paul and Silas came knocking at the back door the next morning before me and Rosebud had time to finish our cinnamon toast and cold sweet milk. He was wearing a fleece-lined cowhide jacket and a hunting cap with the flaps down.

"Brrr," he said, warming his hands over the stove burners.

"How come you be so skinny?" Willie Mae asked.

"Do you think I'm too thin, Miss Willie Mae?" Paul and Silas asked, helping himself to a cup of coffee.

"I know you are. Set over there and lemme fix you something." She was already busy slicing homemade bread and spreading it with butter from Biggie's farm. "You want cinnamon toast or strawberry preserves?" she asked.

"Cinnamon toast, if it's not too much trouble." Paul and

Silas took off his hat and coat and hung them on the back of a chair and sat down, rubbing his hands together.

Just then, Biggie came out of her room wearing the jeans she wears to go fishing and a red plaid shirt that used to belong to my daddy. She had on my old Nikes.

"Give him some preserves, too," she said. "He needs the vitamins. J.R., I've decided you shouldn't go this time. River Street, where Dub lives, isn't a very nice part of town."

"Good," I said. "Then me and Rosebud can put up the outside lights. You promised last year I could get up on the roof and help when I was twelve."

"Well—" Biggie said.

"If you git up there and fall, don't come cryin' to me," Rosebud said.

"I ain't gonna fall!" I said.

"You *are not* going to fall," Biggie said.

"That's what I said, Biggie."

"No, honey, not *ain't*. Are not."

"I are not gonna fall? That ain't right, Biggie."

"J.R.!"

"Yes, ma'am."

"Miss Biggie," Willie Mae said, setting a plate of hot buttered toast in front of Paul and Silas, "did you forget me and Rosebud got to go down to St. Thelma's and take part in the church cleaning today? I told you last week."

"That's okay," I said. "I'll stay home and play video games."

"Sure you'll be all right?" Biggie asked, ruffling my hair with her hand.

"Course. Why does everybody think they have to treat me like a titty baby?"

"Miss Biggie!" Willie Mae said. Something in her tone made me glance up at her, and she was giving Biggie a look I couldn't understand.

"What . . . Oh!" Biggie said. "All right, J.R. I guess you'll have to go with us. And go comb your hair. It's all messy."

Dub's house was covered with gray fake brick siding. The driveway and front yard were full of old wrecked cars. A pit bull tied to a tree watched as we got out of the car. He didn't bark, just strained against his chain and growled way down in his throat as we pushed past the squeaky gate. A shed crammed full of junk was attached to the side of the house and, hanging from the roof, I could see a car engine. Three cages stood on the ground next to the shed, and each held a skinny red rooster. The oldest man I ever saw was sitting in a straight chair on the front porch. He was spitting tobacco into a coffee can, and it ran down his stubbly chin. Dub's feet stuck out from under one of the cars.

Dub rolled out from under the car on a dolly. He was wearing blue coveralls and was covered with grease and dirt.

"Hey, Miss Biggie," he said. "Morn', Paul and Silas." He scrambled up from the dolly. "Reckon you come here to talk about the killin'."

"Just a few questions," Paul and Silas said, "then we'll let you get back to your work. This looks like a seventy-three Mustang. Reckon you can get it in shape?"

Dub stood, wiping his hands on a dirty red rag. "Dunno. Hard to get parts. Come on in the house where we can set."

As we passed the old man, he reached out and pinched Biggie on the behind, then grinned, showing pink gums.

Biggie stopped and looked at him. I thought she was going to belt him a good one, but she only said, "Morning, Cecil."

Dub moved some dirty dishes off the kitchen table and added them to the others in the sink.

"We can set here," he said, giving the table a quick swipe with his rag.

"How've you been, Dub?" Biggie asked. "I haven't seen much of you since you and my boy, Royce, got out of school."

"Yes'm. I'm okay. I hated to hear about Royce. We had some high old times together. This his boy?"

"That's right. J.R. came to live with me after Royce died."

"What you got those roosters for?" I asked.

"Never mind," Biggie said real fast. "We have other things to talk about. Dub, what do you know about Firman's death?"

Dub scratched his head, then examined his fingernails. "Only what I seen, Miss Biggie. And you was there." He grinned. "Somebody sure didn't think much of him, I reckon—shootin' him in the head and pourin' gravy on him."

Paul and Silas looked up. "Who told you he was shot in the head? We didn't know until we got him washed down."

"Oh—uh, well, I seen some blood . . ."

"Never mind," Biggie said. "What time did you arrive at the café, Dub?"

"Umm, lemme see, finished my round and clocked in at the plant at four o'clock. You can check that. Then I come on home and washed up before I picked up Fairy Lee at four-thirty. We must've got to the café around four forty-five or thereabouts."

"Was Firman there then?"

"No'm. Lest he was done dead. And now I think about it, I reckon he was. Was he?"

"Probably," Biggie said. "Did you hear anything? See anything unusual?"

Dub got up and walked around the room. He stopped at the stove. "Ya'll want some coffee? I can make some."

"No, thanks," Biggie said. "Could you answer my question?"

Dub sat down and looked square at Biggie. "Miss Biggie, I was so busy watchin' Fairy Lee, I pure-dee didn't notice nothin' else. Once, my little honey thought she heard something in the kitchen, the teapot, she said. I waited while she went in to check. That's all."

Paul and Silas got up and walked outside, slamming the screen door behind him. Dub watched him go and wiped his face with the red rag, leaving a streak of grease across his cheek.

"What's he doing?" he asked.

"Don't worry," Biggie said. "We're working a murder here. Now, what's this I hear about you stalking Fairy Lee?"

"Who's been tellin' that? Ain't she my wife? Don't a man have a right to keep track of what his wife's up to?"

Biggie patted his hand. "Now don't get upset, honey. I heard Firman was taking her places. That's all."

Dub's face got real red under the dirt. "She says it ain't nothin' to it. She claims he was just friends. You believe that, Miss Biggie?"

55

"I'm sure they were," Biggie said, using the tone of voice she uses when I wake up with a nightmare. "Now, are you and Fairy Lee divorced?"

"Where'd you hear that?"

"But you don't live together?"

"She threw me out, Miss Biggie. Taken her preacher and two old boys from that holiness church of hers over to the house when I was out on a run and moved all my stuff out to the curb. Then she changed all the locks."

"My, my," Biggie said.

"But that's not the crazy part," Dub went on. "Not mor'n a week later she took to callin' me up on the phone—just to talk, she said. Then she took to askin' me over to my own house for supper. Claimed she was scared to stay there by herself. I offered to move back in, but she said no, she had to have time to think and for me to just get her a little gun to keep. Hell, Miss Biggie, I don't know whether I'm married or single."

"You got her the gun?" Biggie asked.

"Yes'm."

"What kind?"

"A little twenty-two revolver. Got it from a pawnshop over in Tyler. Why you reckon she's messin' with me like that, Miss Biggie?"

"I wouldn't worry too much." Biggie stood up. "I imagine she's trying to sort out her feelings for you. Just be patient with her. Now, honey, I want you to let me know if you remember anything else. Anything unusual. It could be important."

"Yes'm, I will."

"And give that old man a bath. He stinks."

"Yes'm."

"It's just a shame," Biggie said as we drove home.

"What, Cousin Biggie?" Paul and Silas asked.

"About Dub," Biggie said. "He went through all twelve grades with my boy, J.R.'s daddy. They were friends. And now look what he's come to."

"But, Biggie," I said, "he works. He's a truck driver. And, Biggie, you always told me it don't matter what a person does, as long as it's honest work."

"That's what I said, and that's what I meant," Biggie said. "Truck driving's honest. Putting innocent creatures into a pit and watching them kill each other is not! Paul and Silas, when this murder is solved, I want you to throw the book at him."

"I plan to, Cousin Biggie. That is to say, if we don't have him in jail for murder. Right now, he looks like our prime suspect."

"Maybe so," Biggie said. "Still, the most obvious person isn't always your killer."

"I know, Cousin Biggie. That's why I took Polaroids of those roosters before we left. They will, no doubt, be moved before the sun goes down today. I got some shots of the dog, too. He had tooth marks all over him."

"Dogfights?"

"Yes. I've heard they go on every Saturday night out at Smoky Hill."

When we got to the square, Biggie said, "Park here, Paul and Silas. I feel like a big chicken-fried steak from the Owl Café."

I love the Owl Café. It's dark and cozy, and Mr. Populus, who owns it, makes the best pies in the whole world.

Butch was sitting at the counter when we got there, having a large slice of apple with ice cream on top. "Ooh," he said, "can I sit with ya'll?"

"Sure, Butch," Biggie said. "Is that your lunch?"

"Yes'm. It's got vitamins in it. Apples are good for you. How's the detecting coming? I never thought I'd say it, but you know, I sort of miss police work—bein' in the fast lane, and all."

Mr. Populus stopped polishing the marble-topped counter and came to take our orders. Me and Biggie ordered the large chicken-fried steak, cut the gravy, and Paul and Silas had the chef's salad.

"What's the talk on the street?" Biggie asked Butch. "About the murder, I mean."

Butch licked the last of his apple pie off his fork. "Well," he said, "the Thripps both think Ben did it so he could run Fresh-as-a-Daisy all by himself. After all, Firman didn't have any other heirs. Of course, Norman, he's so crazy about money he *would* think that way."

"Um-hmm," Biggie said.

Butch counted the names off on his fingers. "Lonie and Julia both agree that it's a crime of passion. They think Dub did it on account of Fairy Lee. Dedrick Plumley down at the drugstore says those Mexicans did it because everybody knows they'll kill just for the fun of it."

Biggie frowned and shook her head. "Shame on Dedrick."

Butch continued like he'd never been interrupted. "Roy Lee Peoples over at the Eazee Freeze says to watch those strangers staying at the Big Eight on account of anybody that would dress up like movie star cowboys might just do anything."

Paul and Silas looked up from his chef's salad and frowned. "That's just downright silly."

"Ruby Muckleroy stopped by the shop yesterday," Butch continued. "She's going around saying that Fairy Lee did it because Firman had been romancing her and promising all kinds of things, but Ruby says a big important man like Firman would never marry some little nobody like Fairy Lee."

"Who told her that?" Biggie asked.

"You'll have to ask her," Butch said, brushing the crumbs off his shirt. "Maybe she made it up. Oh, yeah, Ike Sloan over at the feed store says old man Threadgill might've done it because he's been making threats against the Birdsongs for messing up his creek. Well, I've got to go. You'd never believe how busy I am with Christmas decorations. It seems like everybody in town is wanting wreaths this year. Ta!"

After Butch left, Mr. Populus, who'd been listening as he dried glasses behind the counter, came over to our table.

"Miss Biggie," he said, "is not, I think, Mr. Threadgill who shoots the chicken man."

"Why?" Biggie asked.

"Because he is here bothering my customers from four-twenty to five-fifteen. I am trying to make them leave, but he only shouts insults at me, so I am leaving him alone."

"Thanks, honey." Biggie took a bill out of her purse and dropped it on the table.

Outside, Biggie put her hand on my shoulder. "Let's

walk home. It's a beautiful day now that the wind's died down." She waved good-bye to Paul and Silas. As we walked, she said, "How would you like to go out to the farm tomorrow? It's high time we picked our Christmas tree."

7

The next day, Rosebud backed Biggie's big black car out of the garage so we could all drive out to the farm to get our Christmas tree. Biggie grew up on that farm, but now Monica and her parents, the Sontags, live there. Monica is my best friend even though she is a girl and has hair on only one side of her head on account of being left too close to the fire when she was a baby. Naturally, she was waiting out front with her dog, Buster, when we drove down the bumpy lane that leads from the highway to the farmhouse.

"Hey, J.R. Hey, Rosebud. Hidy, Miss Biggie," she said. "Did ya'll bring a hatchet? Because if you didn't, my daddy's is sharp enough to shave a gnat. Mama said I could go with ya'll."

"Sure, Monica," Biggie said. "You can show us where the best trees are."

"But we don't need your daddy's hatchet," Rose-bud said, taking his chain saw out of the trunk, "we got power."

"Oo-wee," Monica said, "can I run it?"

"Nosirree-bob," Rosebud said. "I ain't gonna be responsible for you sawin' off your 'pendages."

"What are 'pendages,' Rosebud?" I asked.

Rosebud slung the chain saw over his shoulder and started to follow Biggie toward the house. "Why, that's the stuff that hangs off of you—like noses and fingers and stuff. Come on, we ain't got all day."

Biggie had walked to the front porch and stood there chatting with Mrs. Sontag, who is round like an apple.

"Well, you've got a fine day for it," Mrs. Sontag said. "If it was me, I'd hunt down by the creek. Monica got us a dandy one there." She pointed to a cut tree propped against the porch.

"When you going to decorate it?" I asked.

"Tomorrow, I expect," Mrs. Sontag said. "Now, Miss Biggie, when ya'll get through, come on back to the house and have some coffee. I've got sugar cookies in the oven this very minute."

Monica was jumping around like a flea. "Come on," she said. "I know where the best trees are, if you don't mind walking."

We followed Monica past the barn and cow lot where Mr. Sontag keeps his milk cows, then headed south toward the woods that line both sides of Wooten Creek.

"Ya'll want pine or cedar?" Monica asked.

"I think a nice pine," Biggie said. "They're greener."

"I want cedar," I said. "There ain't, I mean aren't, enough branches on a pine—and them old needles get in the way when you hang your ornaments."

"Those," Biggie said. "*Those* needles get in the way."

"That's right, they do," Monica said. "We got cedar for that very reason. They smell awful good, too."

"Okay," Biggie said. "Cedar it is, then. But I want you kids to gather plenty of pine boughs and mistletoe for the house."

It took us a good hour to find the perfect tree. Biggie is very particular. The tree had to be not too tall and not too short, not so bushy that it covered the whole room but not spindly, either. It had to be growing all by itself, so it wouldn't be flat on one side from being next to another tree.

Finally, Rosebud had had enough and parked himself on a mossy rock under a sycamore growing near the creek bank.

"Miss Biggie," he said, "I ain't totin' this chain saw another step. I'll just set right here and when you find your tree, you give a whistle, and I'll come runnin'."

Buster, who had been running in circles around us the whole way, slid down the muddy creek bank and helped himself to a long, cool drink of water. Then he scrambled back up and relieved himself on the trunk of a cedar set off in a little clearing nearby.

"Look!" Monica said, pointing. "Buster's found your tree, Miss Biggie."

Biggie walked all around it and felt the needles. She broke off a little sprig and smelled it.

"Yep," she said, "this is our tree, all right. Rosebud, crank up that saw and let's get it back to the house. I can just taste Ernestine's good coffee and sugar cookies."

Buster didn't run in circles going back, just made a bee-line home with his tail up and his ears back.

"Ain't he smart," Monica said. "He knows he saved the day."

"I guess," I said, remembering the time he'd caused so much trouble falling into a hole last summer. Personally, I think Monica gives that dog a lot more credit than he's entitled to.

Back at the house, Mrs. Sontag poured coffee for the grown-ups and cold milk for me and Monica. Her cookies were almost as good as Willie Mae's. She had cut them out in the shape of Christmas trees and iced them with red and green frosting. She gave us a plateful to take on the front steps to eat.

"Know what?" Monica said, taking a big bite of cookie.

"Yeah, your teeth are all green," I said.

She took a swallow of milk and continued. "We never did get Miss Biggie's mistletoe and pine for the house. I know a place where there's lots, only it's not on our land."

"How far it it?"

"It's too far for walking, but I've got an idea. I'll ask Papa if I can drive the truck over there."

"You drive the truck?" I was jealous. Rosebud never even lets me sit behind the wheel of our car.

"Sure. I drive it all the time. Not on the road, though."

Just then, Mr. Sontag came out to the porch for a chew on account of Mrs. Sontag won't let him chew in the house.

Mr. Sontag is smoke thin and so tall he has to hunch over to go through a door. He flopped down in a chair and pulled a bag of Red Man out of his overalls pocket.

"Papa," Monica said, "Miss Biggie needs some branches and stuff to decorate her house. Can me and J.R. take the truck over to the Birdsong place to cut some?"

Mr. Sontag stuffed a huge wad of tobacco in his mouth. "You'll have to cut across the west pasture," he said. "You know you ain't allowed on the road."

"Come on!" Monica yelled, racing toward the old blue farm truck.

Monica drives like a spooked monkey. My head hit the roof more than once as we bounced across the pasture.

"Watch this!" she shouted and started cutting doughnuts in the field.

"Stop!" I yelled. "I'm getting sick at my stomach."

After that, she straightened the old truck out and we bumped our way to the fence, where she slammed on the brakes, throwing me against the dash.

"We'll have to walk from here," she said, yanking up the emergency brake. "Hand me Papa's hatchet out of the back."

Monica had been right. The property next door was chock-full of green pine trees, and the oak trees were full of mistletoe. Monica started hacking off pine limbs while I shinnied up the oaks, tossing down big hunks of mistletoe.

I held up a big bunch. "Boy hidy," I said. "Would you look at the berries on this stuff?"

"Come on," Monica called, "it's even better farther in."

The woods were getting thicker, and dried briars scratched our arms and faces.

"Don't you think we've got enough?" I said.

"Come on, scaredy-cat," she said. "I know where the best mistletoe in the whole world is."

"What's that smell?" I asked.

"Follow me. I'll show you."

I had a pretty good idea what it was, and I had no desire to see it again, but I followed because it don't do much good to reason with Monica.

Sure enough, pretty soon we came to a draw filled with rotten eggs. The stench was awful, and worse, a flock of buzzards was sitting around making a meal out of those eggs.

"Yuck!" I said.

Monica stood looking with her arms folded and a big grin on her face. "Ain't that something?" she said. "I'll bet you don't have nothing like this in town. Buster! Quit that!"

Old Buster, who had been running along sniffing the ground, had suddenly decided to have a roll in those eggs.

"He sure is a smart dog," I said. "Where's all that good mistletoe you were bragging about?"

"It's right up . . ."

She didn't get a chance to finish because at that moment something whizzed past her ear and hit a pine tree, spraying bark into the air.

"What . . ."

"Gotcha, you lily-livered bandits," a voice said.

I grabbed Monica's hand. "It's old man Threadgill! Run!" I yelled.

I ran as fast as I could, dragging Monica behind. We must have gone a good fifty yards when something happened that turned my blood to clabber. Buster started yelping. The sound of it told me he was hurt bad.

"He's shot my dog!" Monica cried. "J.R., I've got to go back."

I didn't want to risk it, but what could we do? Buster had been hit for sure.

"Get down low," I said.

We crawled back toward the draw that divided the Birdsong property from Threadgill's. I peered through the bushes just in time to see Mr. Threadgill bumping across the pasture toward his house on his old lawn mower, whooping and hollering as he went.

"There's my baby," Monica said. "Oh, he's been shot in the leg. What shall we do, J.R.?"

I poked around until I found an old shingle on the ground. "Slide this under him," I said.

Buster cried a lot, but we finally got him on the shingle, and I carried him through the woods and back to the truck. When we got back to the house, the grown-ups were standing in the yard waiting for us.

"We heard shots," Biggie said.

After we told what had happened, Biggie herded me and Rosebud and Monica and Buster into her car.

"Hurry, Rosebud," she said. "This poor creature's bleeding like a stuck pig."

. . .

When we finally got back home, Willie Mae was just setting a big pan of Aunt Nancy's casserole on the table. If you've never had that, you ought to. It's full of ground meat and noodles and tomatoes and peppers and corn and some more stuff all hid under lots and lots of melted yellow cheese. Willie Mae told me she got the recipe from her Aunt Nancy, who was a powerful voodoo lady from Nacogdoches.

"Set down," she said. "Soon as the bread's ready, we'll eat."

While we ate, we told Willie Mae what had happened.

"Dr. Furr took the bullet out," Biggie said, dropping the slug on the tablecloth. "He said Buster will get well, but he may be a little gimpy."

"Biggie," I said, "you told me that old man only carried a toy pistol."

"I thought it was a toy," Biggie said.

"Always was before," Rosebud said. "How come you reckon he's all of a sudden got himself a real gun?"

"I don't know," Biggie said, "but I aim to make it my business to find out."

Willie Mae popped a piece of homemade French bread in her mouth. "So," she said, "you didn't get no Christmas tree? Or no greenery for the house?"

I slapped my forehead. "Oh, no! And tomorrow's the first Sunday in Advent."

"Never mind," Rosebud said, smacking his lips over his last bite of casserole. "I'll shoot out there first thing in the morning. You'll have your tree by the time you wake up."

"Good!" Biggie said, patting my hand. "And you can climb the ladder and put the star on top."

"And I'm gonna make you some rocky road fudge to eat while you're doing it," Willie Mae said.

I wondered why everybody was being so nice to me.

8

The next day was Sunday. We decorated Biggie's house for Christmas.

We'd all helped trim the tree and arrange the greenery, draping pine limbs and red velvet bows on the mantel and over the stair rail. While Butch helped Biggie make a centerpiece for the dining room table and Willie Mae stirred up some hot apple cider in the kitchen, me and Rosebud sat on the floor in front of the tree and discussed what we wanted for Christmas.

"What would you want, Rosebud," I asked, "if money was no object—you could have anything in the whole world?"

Rosebud lay back on the carpet with his hands behind his head and thought for the longest time. Finally he spoke. "I'd get my little sweetie a pair of solid gold earrings, great old big ones."

"How come? Willie Mae don't even wear jewelry except her grandmere's gold cross."

"She used to. She used to have these big shiny loops she wore in her ears ever single day of her life."

"What happened to them?"

Rosebud raised up and sat cross-legged on the floor. "Pass me that plate of rocky road, and I'll tell you." After he'd chewed his candy, he continued. "We was living in New Iberia back then. I was working for old man Theriot, crabbing. Willie Mae took in washing and conjured a little on the side. We were making it, but just barely. Wellsir, one morning early, me and Mr. Theriot and Mr. Theriot's boy, Petey, taken the pirogue out to set some traps. Hotamighty, cher, was it foggy! Couldn't see a gator if he was settin' on your foot."

"Wow," I said, "was it scary?"

"Scary? Naw. Shoot, me and them had been out in that swamp a hundred times or more. You just had to keep your eyes open case a water moccasin taken a notion to drop off one of them trees into the boat. I had my shotgun along just in case, though. Well, Mr. Theriot was polin' the pirogue while I watched for gators and snakes. Little Petey, he was just about your age, was leanin' over the side of the boat tryin' to see if he could spot any turtles swimmin' by. First thing you know, Petey had done leaned too far and fell right smack in the bayou. Oh, me, oh, my, Mr. Theriot let out a holler. 'My boy!' he yelled. 'Save my boy!' 'Fore I give it a thought, I'd jumped in after him. I got my hand on the kid, but he panicked and stared thrashin' and fightin' me."

"Oo-wee," I said.

71

Rosebud reached for the candy dish and poked around looking for the biggest piece. Finally he selected one and popped it in his mouth. Then I had to wait until he chewed and swallowed.

"So, what happened?" I asked.

"Oh. Well, all that thrashin' had got the attention of a big papa gator who happened to be having his nap in amongst the cypress knees near the bank. He swum over our way and opened his big old mouth . . . wide. I could see all the way down his gullet."

"What'd you do?"

"Go in the kitchen and get me a drink of water, and I'll tell you."

When I came back with the water, Rosebud took up where he'd left off.

"So, then, I seen that old gator rollin' his eyes toward the boy, who had finally quit fightin' and was hangin' on to my shirt, bellerin' like a banshee. Slowly, that old gator fanned his tail and swiveled hisself around in the water 'til his mouth was over the boy and ready to bust that kid in half with one bite. Well, I had to think fast. What I done was, I rolled between the two of them, grabbed a gig outta the boat, and rammed it right down that old gator's throat."

"Did it kill him?"

"Naw, just made him mad. Then he taken after me. Mr. Theriot had done reached down and pulled the boy back in the boat. I rassled that old gator with all my might, but I was gettin' wore out. It was then I noticed blood flowin' out in the water—and it wasn't no gator blood. With the last bit of strength I had, I grabbed the gig out of his mouth and rammed it into the soft skin under his throat. He took one last snap at me and swum off, draggin' Mr. Theriot's gig with him. When they drug me outta the water, we seen I'd been dern near filleted. That gator had bit me bad acrost the chest and shoulder. Want to see?"

Quick as a minute, Rosebud unbuttoned his shirt and showed me his scar. It was shiny and V-shaped and ran from his right shoulder halfway down his chest.

"Golly," I said, "that's some story. You were a hero, Rosebud."

"Yeah."

"But I still don't see what that's got to do with you wanting to buy earrings for Willie Mae for Christmas."

"You don't?" Rosebud said. "Well, I couldn't do no work for more'n a month, and Willie Mae had to sell her grandmere's gold earrings to buy food. Ever since then, I been just waitin' 'til the day I had the money to . . ."

Just then, Willie Mae came in carrying a tray full of hot apple cider and rum balls. "Huh," she said, "how come you be showin' off that scar?"

Rosebud buttoned his shirt and got real busy with the lights on the tree.

"I would've thought you'd be proud of him, Willie Mae," I said. "Saving that little boy and all."

"What's he been tellin' you? He got that scar in a razor fight down on Chartres Street. It was over a crap game, as I recollect." She set the tray down on the coffee table. "That was the night I said good-bye to my grandmere's gold earrings." She turned and walked back to the kitchen.

Later that afternoon, I was reading *Goosebumps* in my room when a car door slammed and someone rang our doorbell. I went to the stair to see who was here because, as Biggie says, I'm curiouser than a coon in the kitchen. Biggie opened the door, and who should be standing there but those Culpeppers. My stomach did the hokey-pokey while I leaned over the banister to hear what they were saying.

"We've come to take J.R. on a little outing," my other grandmother said.

Skinny stood with his hands in his pockets, whistling through his teeth.

"Well, that depends . . ." Biggie said.

"Depends ain't nothing but a diaper," Jane Culpepper said. "You can't say 'depends' to me because I've got a piece of paper saying I can take him anytime I please. And right now, I plan to take him on a little outing."

I could hear Biggie's false teeth click as she shut her mouth with a snap. I figured those Culpeppers were in for it now, but all she said was "You'll have to ask him if he wants to go."

"He'll go, all right. Just get him down here."

I trotted back to my room and was pretending to be reading when Biggie came in and closed the door behind her.

"You heard?" she said. You can't fool Biggie.

"Yes'm."

"Well?"

"I don't want to go."

"Then you'd better come down and tell them."

The Culpeppers were both dressed in white. Jane wore a pair of white jeans, too tight, with a white suede vest with fringe, over a blue denim shirt. She had on a white Stetson and white boots with silver inlays. Skinny had on a white western suit.

Jane grabbed me and hugged me to her. She smelled like french fries. "Howdy, little buckaroo. Your grampy and me came to take you on a little outing. Get your jacket. It's nippy out."

Skinny grinned and pulled a quarter out of my ear.

"That's nothing," I said. "I've seen that done a hundred times."

"J.R., don't be rude," Biggie said.

Skinny just grinned again and pulled a live mouse out of my ear and handed him to me.

"Wow," I said, "can I keep him?"

Skinny nodded, and I slipped him in my shirt pocket.

"Well, get your jacket," Jane said. "We gotta get going."

"I can't go," I said. "I'm pretty busy right now."

"Well, that's that," Biggie said, closing the door. "You folks take care, you hear?"

Jane Culpepper pushed the door open and whispered something in my ear.

"Okay," I said. "I'll get my jacket." I handed my mouse to Biggie. "Keep him 'til I get back, okay?"

I looked back as I walked to the car between the Culpeppers. Biggie was standing in the doorway holding my mouse with an expression on her face I couldn't read. It was a mixture of sad and puzzled and really, really mad. I figured I was in for it when I got home, but those Culpeppers had made me an offer I couldn't refuse.

We drove to the mall in Center Point. Over the music of Bob Wills and the Texas Playboys on the radio, Jane told me all about the dude ranch they owned in Montana. She said they had not only dogs and horses and cattle but exotic animals too.

"What kind of exotic animals?" I asked.

"Oh, emus and zebras and llamas. Stuff like that," she said. "We've got baby ostriches, too. Fresh out of the eggs."

"Would I be able to play with them?" I asked.

"Well, sure. You can have one for your very own—for a pet," she said.

When we got to the mall, we went straight to the big sporting goods store and headed for the bicycle department. They must have had a thousand bicycles in there, but I passed most of them up. I knew exactly what I wanted.

"Take your choice," Jane said. "How about this nice red one?"

"Um, no," I said.

Skinny was walking beside me with his hand on my shoulder. He pointed to a rack of iridescent blue ones.

"Nope," I said. "Over here's the one I want."

I had spotted a Dyno VFR sitting all by itself. It was shiny black with lots of chrome.

"Oh, that's just an old black one," Jane said. "How 'bout this nice green one?"

It took a while, but I finally made them understand that I'd wanted a Dyno VFR practically my whole entire life. Skinny paid cash for it, and we put it in the trunk of the car and headed back to Job's Crossing.

"Skinny's hungry," Jane said. "Where's the best place to get a milk shake?"

"The Eazee Freeze," I said.

Roy Lee Peoples, the owner, was sitting on a stool playing his guitar and singing "Mule Train" to entertain his customers. When he saw the Culpeppers, he stopped playing and put his guitar back in its case.

"What can I get for you folks?" he said, not smiling.

We ordered milk shakes. I had two, then a dilly bar for dessert.

"Can I go home now?" I asked. "I want to ride my new bike."

Back at Biggie's house, Skinny unloaded the bike and put the handlebars in my hands. He ruffled my hair. Jane gave me another big old stinky hug, and they drove off in their car, honking "The Eyes of Texas" as they went.

At supper that night, Willie Mae asked, "How come you ain't eatin' your supper?"

"I think I'm too tired from riding my new bike," I said.

"Tired never kept you from eatin' fried chicken, boy," Rosebud said. "What'd them people feed you?"

"I don't feel too good," I said. "I think I'll go to bed."

When I got to my room, I saw that Rosebud had put my mouse in my old hamster cage and given it food and water. It was racing around in the little squeaky wheel. I was just getting ready to crawl into bed when Biggie came in. Not many people know it, but she still tucks me in at night.

"How was your day?" she asked.

"I dunno," I said, wondering why I was feeling the way I did.

"That's a mighty nice bike they bought you," she said.

"Yes'm."

Biggie tucked the covers around me, gave me a kiss, and turned out the light as she left the room.

That dern mouse kept me awake most of the night.

9

"I agree, Lonie," Biggie said. "It was a crime of passion because of the insult to the body."

Biggie had invited the Daughters over for the afternoon to make Christmas ornaments to sell at the bazaar. Butch had come with Miss Mattie because, I guess, he didn't have anything better to do. The big round table in Biggie's sunroom was piled with paint, scraps of felt, ribbons, glitter, and a bunch of other junk. I was sitting on the wicker settee listening to them talk while I played with the glop I'd made with starch and white glue.

"Thee, Ruby, I told you tho," Miss Lonie said. "That old dirty Dub did it because he'th burned up with jealouthy over hith little wife, Fairy Lee."

"Humph!" Mrs. Muckleroy said. "I still say greed was the motive. I'm putting my money on Ben Birdsong.

He killed Firman so he'd have Fresh-as-a-Daisy all to himself."

Miss Julia Lockhart put down the little bitty stocking she was knitting and took a sip of tea. "That could have been a crime of passion," she said. "Ben always was jealous of Firman. I know because my little sister, Betty Lou, went to school with those two."

"Brother Birdsong and his wife always did favor Firman," Mrs. Moody said. "He used to be real handsome before he let himself go. Remember, Biggie?"

Biggie nodded.

"That's right," Miss Mattie said. "Pass me that green paint, Butch. As I recall, after he came back from his midlife-crisis trip, that's when he got so fat. He used to dress real nice and even lifted weights to stay trim."

"Brother Birdthong wath fat," Miss Lonie said. "It runth in the family."

Miss Julia lowered her voice and leaned in toward the others. "I heard he was having an *affair* with that little waitress," she said.

"I don't believe it," Mrs. Moody said. "Her mother used to do sewing for me."

"Essie," Miss Mattie said, "what makes you think the girl couldn't be having an affair with Firman Birdsong just because her mother used to sew for you? That's the silliest thing I ever heard."

Mrs. Moody looked hurt. "You didn't let me finish. They belong to that Jesus church out on Center Point Road. You know, those people are real moral. They don't even use makeup—let alone have affairs!"

"Ya'll like this?" Butch asked, holding up a corn husk angel he'd made.

"Ooh, yeth," Miss Lonie said. "Butch, you're tho talented!"

"I always could work with my hands," Butch said.

"Did you have to put so much makeup on it?" Mrs. Muckleroy asked. "It looks like a, well, you know, one of *those* women. . . ."

"A hooker," Miss Julia said. "My Lord, Ruby, spit it out. This is the nineties. You'll hear worse than that on TV while you're eating your supper!"

"We never keep television on while we eat," Mrs. Muckleroy said. "Curtis won't hear of it."

"I heard Firman had promised to deed Fairy Lee half interest in the restaurant," Mrs. Moody said.

"I heard he'd proposed to her," Miss Julia said. "That just proves what my mama always said, 'There's no fool like an old—' "

"Well, if you ask me," Miss Mattie interrupted, "the girl never had a chance. Her daddy roughnecked, so naturally they moved around a lot when she was little. What I heard was, he just took off one day and never came back." She looked at me. "The child couldn't have been any older than J.R. here."

"But developed for her age," Mrs. Moody said. "I remember when her mama'd bring her to the house while she sewed . . ."

"Some of them just bloom early," Mrs. Muckleroy said. "I heard they'd have been out on the street if Ben Birdsong hadn't given them a company house to live in."

"He hired the mother to pluck chickens in the plant, too," Miss Mattie said. "I always thought Ben had his eyes on her—the mother, I mean."

"Mattie! Thame on you," Miss Lonie said. "Ben'th a deacon in the church."

"Grow up, Lonie," Miss Julia said, then turned to Biggie. "Fairy Lee's just an innocent country girl. She couldn't have been more than fifteen when she married Dub. What I think is, Firman just swept her off her feet—with his money, and all."

Biggie set down the wooden Santa she'd been working on. It was a mess. She wiped her hands on a towel.

"I was thinking," she said, "since we were all there at the restaurant that night, why don't we put our heads together and see whether we can remember anything that might shed some light on the crime?" She looked at Miss Lonie first.

"I wath watching that Dub," Miss Lonie said. "He didn't take hith eythth off Fairy Lee for one thecond. I think he'th real mean looking." She shuddered. "And he'th *tattooed!*"

"That's nothing," Miss Mattie said. "Norman's got a little teeny tattoo of an anchor. He got it in the Navy."

"Ooh, I've never seen it," Butch said. "Where?"

"In San Diego, I think," Miss Mattie said. "The boys were on shore leave—"

"Not that! Where on him?" Butch said.

Miss Mattie glared at him. "That's none of your business. But if I told you, you'd all know what a brave man my husband is!"

"What about you, Butch?" Biggie said real fast. "See anything odd?"

Butch squeezed his eyes shut. "Well, first of all, the place was real tacky. I mean, who would put gray floors and walls with blue and yellow curtains. And did you notice the booths and tabletops? Army green. I mean, really!"

"Butch . . ." Biggie said.

"Oh, well, okay. I did happen to notice Ben Birdsong go into the kitchen and stay an awful long time. That was right soon after he came by our table to visit. I was waiting for him to come out so I could ask him who his decorator was."

Biggie gave up.

"How about you, Ruby?" she asked.

"Not a thing!" Mrs. Muckleroy said. "We were stuck off in the back room because we got there late. Coming in, though, I did see that crazy old Clovis Threadgill pointing his toy gun at those peculiar people staying at the Big Eight. He was calling them all kinds of names, too. He should be locked up before he hurts somebody."

"He's harmless," Miss Julia said.

"What time was that?" Biggie asked.

"Around six-thirty, I suppose," Mrs. Muckleroy said. "We had to park clear over at the Nazarene Church parking lot."

Just then, Willie Mae came in with a tray of Christmas goodies and set it on the coffee table in front of me. She glared at my ball of glop.

"Git that stuff off Miss Biggie's cushions," she said.

"Where's Rosebud?"

"Gone to the store for me. Now, git on."

I put my glop back in its plastic bag and stuffed it in my pocket. I went outside and sat on the back steps. Prissy Moody was running back and forth inside her fence and barking at me. I chunked a pebble at her, but it hit a picket and bounced back in our yard. I wondered why Biggie seemed more interested in finding a killer than saving me, her only blood kin, from having to go live in Montana with strangers. The way I saw it, since she'd said they couldn't leave town until the murder was solved, she shouldn't be trying so hard to solve the dern murder. Didn't she realize when they left, I'd have to go, too? Well, I thought, if she didn't want to keep me, I'd show her a thing or two.

I slipped through the back screen and got my jacket off a kitchen chair. I hopped on my new bike and made a bee-line for the Big Eight Motel. Might as well visit my new grandparents, I thought. Maybe I'd learn to like them. I kind of already like him a little on account of he didn't talk your head off, and he could do magic. Also, I was thinking about the baby ostrich they'd said I could have.

Their car wasn't parked in front of their room, but I knocked on the door, just in case. Nobody answered, so I peeked in the window. Nobody was home. I found a dollar and some change left from my lunch money in my jacket pocket, so I decided to stop in at Fresh-as-a-Daisy for a Big Red. Two truckers were sitting at the counter drinking coffee. I took a seat at the far end.

Fairy Lee came out of the kitchen carrying two chicken finger baskets and set them in front of the truckers.

"Hey, J.R.," she said. "What can I get you?"

"I'll take a Big Red and a Snickers," I said.

Fairy Lee took my drink out of the cooler, wiped it with a towel, and pulled my candy bar out from under the glass case where the cash register sits.

"How come you to be so far from home?" she asked.

I told her I'd come to see the Culpeppers.

"They left early this morning."

"Left? You mean moved out?"

"Nope. Just left. They didn't take their bags or nothin'. I heard all about her being your other grandma."

"Uh-huh."

"She was in here sayin' she's takin' you home with her. You goin'?"

"Maybe."

Fairy Lee patted her big old hair and looked at the truckers. "Ya'll doin' all right?" she said.

They nodded and went on eating their food.

"They been comin' here for breakfast ever since they got to town," she said to me. "Yesterday they left me three whole dollars for a tip."

"Were you in love with Mr. Firman Birdsong?" I asked, just to change the subject.

Fairy Lee turned red as a fox's butt at pokeberry time. "How come you to ask me that?"

"I heard you were. I heard you and him were talking about gettin' married. I heard he was givin' you half this café, even."

"Well, you—" Just then, the bell over the door tinkled, and Fairy Lee grabbed me by the wrist and squeezed hard. "Shh!" she hissed.

When I looked around, I saw Dub come through the door. He took a seat in the corner booth on the side by the motel. Fairy Lee gave my wrist a hard pinch, then went over and squeezed into the booth beside him. They put

85

their heads together and commenced talking. I finished my drink and laid my money on the counter, making sure to leave a dime for Fairy Lee.

I went outside and walked around to the back of the building. Maybe I'd find a clue that would solve the murder; then the Culpeppers would leave, and I'd go with them. I guessed Biggie would feel mighty bad when she saw me riding out of town in that big orange car with the horn playing "The Eyes of Texas Are Upon You."

The ground was soft where the pavement ended, making it easy for me to see a bunch of narrow tracks. I figured they must have been made by Mr. Threadgill's riding mower. I walked all around the back of the building, examining the ground for footprints or maybe a bloody trail that would lead me to the killer's hideout. I looked and looked, but there was no bloody trail, and the only footprints I saw led from the kitchen door to the Dumpster.

I sat down on the ground with my back against the steel Dumpster to think things over. While I was thinking, I pulled my glop out and started playing with it to relax myself. Before long, I heard the kitchen door slam. It startled me so bad I dropped my glop on the ground. I peered around the side of the Dumpster and saw it was only one of Mr. Birdsong's Mexican chefs dragging a sack of trash. After he went back in the kitchen, I picked up my glop, brushed the grass and dirt off it, and put it back in the bag. I wasn't doing too good as a detective. Besides, it was getting cold. I decided I might as well go home and see what Willie Mae was fixing for supper.

By the time I got back to our house, the sun was low in the sky and the tree shadows looked like skinny arms reaching across the front yards along our block. As I wheeled my bike into the garage, I saw Biggie and Rosebud through the lighted kitchen window. They were sitting at the table drinking coffee and watching Willie Mae at the stove. I wondered how many more times I'd come home to Biggie's hugs and Rosebud's tall tales and Willie Mae's good-smelling kitchen.

I walked in just in time to see Willie Mae take a pan of crawfish pie out of the oven. She looked at me over her shoulder.

"Look at you," she said. "Set down here by the stove and git warm. Where you been?"

"Nowhere," I said and flopped down on a chair.

"Hold your horses," Biggie said. "First, take off your jacket and wash your hands. After supper, we're all going into the den and watch *It's a Wonderful Life.*"

When I came back in the kitchen, Willie Mae had set a bowl of spinach salad on the table beside a loaf of her good homemade French bread. It smelled good, and I realized I was hungry enough to eat a Mexican saddle.

"Come on. It's time for the movie," Biggie said as I was sopping up the last of the crawfish gravy from my plate. "We'll all pitch in and do the dishes after it's over."

Personally, I think *It's a Wonderful Life* is a dumb movie. I'd rather watch *The Grinch,* but I knew I was outnumbered, so I sat on the floor and pulled out my glop. I was stretching it into a rope between my hands when something fell out and hit my foot. I picked it up and examined it.

"Biggie!" I said.

"Be quiet, J.R. This is the good part," Biggie said. "I just love that old angel, Clarence."

"But, Biggie . . ."

Biggie ignored me until I crawled over to her chair and held the thing I'd found between her eyes and the television.

"J.R.! Quit that . . . oh, my stars. Where did you get this?"

"It fell out of my glop."

"Turn on the overhead light so I can see."

Rosebud got up and stood by Biggie's chair.

"My, oh, me," he said, "what do you know about that. A twenty-two shell."

"J.R., how did this get in your glop?" Biggie asked.

Naturally, she made me tell how I'd gone to see the Culpeppers and they weren't home and so I'd decided to do a little detecting of my own. I told about how I'd dropped my glop on the ground behind the Dumpster.

Biggie looked at me funny but didn't say a word about me riding my bike to the bypass, which is strictly against the rules. All she said was "This may be a crucial piece of evidence."

Later, when she came to tuck me in, Biggie said, "J.R., why did you want to see the Culpeppers? I thought you didn't like them."

I turned my face to the wall and wouldn't answer.

"J.R."

I still wouldn't answer.

Finally she kissed me on the cheek and left the room. It was a long time before I heard her footsteps going back down the hall.

10

The next day, I had plans to ride my new bike to a place I know behind the school grounds where me and a bunch of guys had made a dirt track, but Biggie had other plans. She said because I was the one that found the .22 shell, I had to go with her to show it to Paul and Silas.

Paul and Silas first showed up in Job's Crossing last year. He came riding into town on a big Harley, wearing black leather and looking tough. Believe me, we were all pretty surprised when he turned out to be Biggie's cousin from Tennessee that she'd never met. He told us his mother took his name from an old-timey church song. After he rescued me and Monica from some kidnappers the night of the Pioneer Days Festival, he rode off on his motorcycle to seek his fortune. We thought we'd most likely seen the last of him until he appeared at our front door one day dressed in a green plaid suit and carrying a white plastic sample case with shiny brass buckles. He said he'd given up biking for good and decided to start a new career as a businessman.

"I wasn't cut out to be a road warrior," he said.

"So, what kind of business did you choose?" Biggie asked.

"The construction business. Vinyl siding, trim work, and roofing. Could I interest you in new siding for your home?" He opened his case. "You can see, I have every color and style a person could desire. Personally, I think your house would look stunning in forest green with mustard trim. Cover your home with Wooten's Woodgrain Vinyl, and you'll never paint again."

Biggie's eyes opened wide. "Wooten's! You're calling this stuff *Wooten's*?"

"Yes, ma'am. A fine name for a fine product."

Now, if you lived in Job's Crossing, you'd know that Biggie is right proud of her family name on account of her ancestor, James Royce Wooten, who settled this town. If Paul and Silas had known her the way I do, he'd have seen what was coming.

"J.R.," she said, "run out to the kitchen and ask Willie Mae to make a fresh pitcher of tea. See if she's got any of that chess pie left from dinner." She turned to Paul and Silas. "Are you making any money, honey?"

When I came back, he had closed his sample case and was sitting facing Biggie, his hands hanging between his legs.

"I guess I'm just a failure, Cousin Biggie," he said. "First, I couldn't make it as a denizen of the open road. Now nobody wants to buy my siding."

"Naturally," Biggie said. "It's tacky."

"I know."

"Tell you what. You just go get your things and move into my garage apartment. We'll find something for you that's fit for a Wooten. Have you ever thought about police work?"

"Never."

"Well, it so happens that we have an opening for a police chief right here in Job's Crossing, and I think you'd be perfect for the job."

"Sadly, I must decline," he said, "for you see, Cousin Biggie, though it shames me to say it, the unflinching valor that has been the mainstay of countless generations of proud Wooten men has passed me by. I would be a failure as an officer of the law owing to the fact that I am a hopeless coward."

Biggie patted his knee. "Never mind, honey. All you've got to do is issue a few parking tickets and make sure Clovis Threadgill doesn't ride his lawn mower on the sidewalk. J.R. could handle the job."

I could have told him his goose was cooked. The next day, Biggie went downtown, moved Butch, our acting chief, out of the police station, and moved Paul and Silas in. After a while, I think he started to like the job. That is, before Firman Birdsong got murdered.

When me and Biggie got to town, we found Paul and Silas standing in front of Plumley's drugstore talking to Mr. Plumley. Mr. Plumley is a little bitty man who always wears gray suits with starched white shirts and black bow ties. Mostly, when he talks, it's barely above a whisper. But today he was shouting, and his face was red as a baboon's rear end.

"What I don't understand," he said, shaking his tiny fist under Paul and Silas's nose, "is why the city can't give me a free parking permit in front of my own store. It's cutting way into my profits—having to come out here every hour to put another nickel in this gosh-derned meter. It's unconstitutional, is what it is!"

Paul and Silas looked at Biggie and shrugged his shoulders.

"Put away your ticket book," Biggie said. "Dedrick, go inside and get a paper sack to cover this meter. I'll take care of the city council. Get in the car, Paul and Silas, we've got things to do."

Biggie drove the car to the Fresh-as-a-Daisy café and parked in the rear.

"Now," she said to me, "show us exactly where you dropped your glop."

I showed them where I'd been sitting behind the Dumpster. Biggie poked around the area looking for clues. She followed Mr. Threadgill's mower tracks, which ran from the front of the building to where they circled the Dumpster, then disappeared in the grass beyond.

"Yoo-hoo!" a voice called.

I looked up and saw Jane Culpepper hobbling across the rutty ground in her high-heeled boots. She was wearing a sky blue cowgirl dress with white fringe.

"What'chall doing?" she asked.

Biggie glanced at her. "Afternoon, Jane," was all she said.

My other grandmother walked up to Biggie and shoved her face in Biggie's. "I believe I asked you a question," she said. "I believe I just politely inquired what the hell you was doing, on account of I was curious why you'd let *my* grandson play around this here nasty old Dumpster."

Biggie's eyes flashed, but she didn't say a word, just moved around Jane and kept on examining the ground for clues.

Jane Culpepper moved in front of Biggie again. She was mad, I could tell, because her fringe was dancing around her chest like a drunk spider.

"I reckon my daughter was right," she said. "You're nothing but a ignorant fool that don't know the first thing about raising kids."

I backed off to watch. Biggie's no bigger than a minute, but if you ever get her riled, watch out. She can be dangerous as a scorpion in an outhouse. I was waiting for her to give Jane the tongue-whipping of her life. Boy, was I surprised when Biggie just stepped away and kept right on searching the ground.

That was more than old Jane could take. She commenced jumping up and down and shouting, "You think you're something special, doncha? Well, you're not. You're just a crazy old woman that lives with two crazy old niggers! I've got a good mind to take my grandson and hightail it back to Montana this very day!"

Biggie had been bending over some tracks on the ground. Now she stood up real slow, looking at Jane. Paul and Silas must have seen the look in her eyes, because he suddenly stepped between the two and grabbed Jane by the arm.

"Madam," he said, "you're not permitted to leave town

until this murder has been solved. You'd be wise to return to your motel room before I am forced to take you into custody for disturbing the peace."

She argued and squawked and cussed enough to singe the grass around her until, finally, Paul and Silas grabbed her by the arm and commenced pulling her back toward the motel. Then I saw Skinny come out of their room, whistling through his teeth. He took her arm and led her back into the room and closed the door.

There goes my baby ostrich, I thought. I knew I'd just been kidding myself, thinking I could live with those two. I wasn't about to go off with any old woman that called Biggie and Rosebud and Willie Mae bad names, even if she was my rightful legal grandmother and had a piece of paper saying so.

Biggie was staring from the Dumpster to the kitchen window. "Let's go inside the café and have some cocoa," she said, just like nothing had happened. "I'm right chilly."

We followed her into the warm café. The air smelled like coffee and french fries.

After Fairy Lee had brought us hot mugs of cocoa, Biggie took a sip, then said, "How many people connected with this case have twenty-two revolvers? It seems to me like they're getting common as pig tracks around here."

"Biggie," I said, "old man Threadgill's got a real gun. Remember, he shot at me and Monica."

"I remember, honey," she said. "Paul and Silas, you're going to have to go out there and confiscate that gun."

"Me?" Paul and Silas looked pale. "Cousin Biggie, he'd shoot me before I could open my mouth. The old fellow's so used to firing off shots with his toy gun, he doesn't know the difference."

"You're probably right, honey," Biggie said. "But we can't let him keep it. Anyway, we need a shell from it to send to the ballistics lab for comparison with the one you found."

"I know, Biggie," I said. "We could go out to Monica's place and look on the ground where he was shooting at us."

"You don't understand, J.R.," she said. "The shells from a revolver don't drop on the ground the way they do from your daddy's squirrel gun. They stay in the cylinder. We have to have that gun."

"Then, Biggie, why . . ."

"Let's see," Biggie said, "who else has a twenty-two? Oh, I know." She raised her voice. "Fairy Lee, come over here, please."

Fairy Lee had been standing beside the jukebox flipping through the selections. She stuck a quarter in and pressed a button, then hurried over to our table as the music started playing.

"Do ya'll like Emmylou Harris?" she asked. "I just think she has the sweetest voice. Mama don't much like me listening to secular music, but even she don't mind Emmylou too much."

"Sit down a minute, honey," Biggie said, "and tell me all about that gun Dub got for you. I believe he said it was a twenty-two revolver."

"Yes'm, it is, and I'm scared to death of the thing."

"Where do you keep it?" Biggie asked.

Fairy Lee pointed toward the counter. "It's right over there. In my purse. You want to see it, Miss Biggie?"

Fairy Lee dug underneath the counter and came back carrying a cloth tote bag with teddy bears printed all over it. She stuck her hand in the bag and came out with a plastic zip bag, the kind Biggie keeps her face powder and lipstick in. She opened the zipper and pulled out a little blue steel revolver no bigger than Rosebud's hand. Using one finger, she slid it across the table toward Biggie.

"Did you know you have to have a permit to carry one of these?" Paul and Silas asked.

"No, sir," Fairy Lee said.

"I'll have to confiscate this weapon, Miss Fairy Lee. If you'll stop by the police station, I'll tell you how to start the paperwork for a permit."

Fairy Lee shook her head. "I don't want the old thing. It was all Dub's idea. He's one of them gun nuts, I call em . . . you know, always talking about the right to bear arms. You ought to see all the guns and other stuff he's got stored out behind his house. I bet he could start his own army if he was to take a notion to. I finally took to carrying this thing just to shut him up."

"You don't say," Biggie said. "Well, it's almost lunchtime. Willie Mae's making purple hull peas, smothered steak with onions, and cornbread. You want to eat with us, Paul and Silas?"

Paul and Silas emptied the cylinder of the gun and dropped the shells in his shirt pocket. Then he stuck the gun in his belt. He said he couldn't have lunch with us on account of he'd joined the Rotary Club, and they were having their meeting in the back room of the Owl Café.

"I hope you'll give me a rain check," he said.

When we got home, Rosebud was sitting at the kitchen table with parts to Biggie's toaster spread in front of him.

"Somebody done put a piece of fruitcake in this thing," he said, looking at me. "Miss Biggie, I think you're gonna have to get a new one."

I picked up Booger and headed up the back stairs to my room. As I left, I heard Willie Mae say, "Miss Biggie, that Ben Birdsong's been phonin' you all morning. He says it's very important, and you're to call him as soon as you get back."

"I will," Biggie said, "but first I'm going to have my lunch and a little nap. I declare, one of these days, that Jane Culpepper's going to push me too far."

When I got to my room, I dug to the back of my sock drawer and pulled out the spare sock I kept my life savings in. I dumped it out in a pile on my bed, pushing Booger away on account of he thought it was a game and started in knocking my money all over the place. I put all my dimes and nickels and quarters in little piles and counted them. I now had $92.00. I put my money away, figuring I'd have to get more if I was to carry out my plan. I got out my school notebook and started writing down ways I could make more money. I wrote:

1. sell my old bike
2. rake leaves
3. beg from Biggie

Number 3 would be the hardest because Biggie always has to know everything. You have to get up pretty early in the morning to get money out of Biggie without telling her why you want it. I'd have to think of something, though, because I knew now that running away from home was my only chance of escaping those evil Culpeppers.

11

The next morning Biggie came into my room without even knocking.

"Get up, honey," she said. "It's bazaar day. Remember? You've got to help Rosebud carry boxes over to the fellowship hall at the Methodist church."

I rolled over and put my head under my pillow. Booger crawled under the down comforter and curled up by my feet. He wasn't ready to get up, either. Biggie gave my toe a yank.

"Umph," I said.

"Get up," Biggie said, "before I send Rosebud up here to tickle you."

I wanted to go back to sleep. I'd been dreaming about my plan to run away. I dreamed I'd set up housekeeping in Betty Jo Darling's old abandoned cabin in the woods across Wooten Creek. I was living on squirrel meat and wild plums and fish I'd caught from the creek. Monica was there with me, cleaning house and cooking up the food I brought home. This could only happen in a dream, because Monica'd told me a long time ago that she'd never cook and clean for any man. She said she was going to join the army to be a paratrooper and never ever get married.

"J.R., hurry up," Biggie said, coming back in my room. "We need you."

"Will I get paid?" I asked from under the pillow.

"I guess so. Sure. You'll need some extra money for Christmas shopping." She leaned down and kissed my cheek. "Now get dressed. Willie Mae's making blueberry waffles." She turned and hurried out of the room.

I sat up and pulled my old comforter over my shoulders. It was white with little blue ducks, and I'd slept with it for almost my whole entire life. I'd take that with me. I couldn't live off the land without my down comforter. After a little while, I crawled out of bed and got dressed. At least I wasn't working for free this time. I'd need all the cash I could save for when I was on my own. I thought about my dream. Maybe I *would* just go out and live on the creek. Betty Jo's cabin was snug and had a woodstove for heat. And I knew it was empty on account of Betty Jo and her kids had moved to a house in town just this past fall.

I was digging on the floor of my closet for my red flannel shirt when Rosebud walked in.

"Willie Mae says rattle your hocks or she's unpluggin' the waffle iron," he said.

I found my shirt and followed Rosebud down to the

kitchen. About a million cardboard boxes were piled by the back door.

"We've got to move all that?" I asked.

"They ain't heavy. Now, eat up," Willie Mae said, setting a plate of crispy waffles in front of me. "You want powdered sugar or ribbon cane?"

"Powdered sugar," I said, "and lots of butter."

When me and Rosebud arrived at the fellowship hall with the first load, Biggie was already there helping the ladies set up folding tables along the sides of the room. Mrs. Muckleroy and Miss Mattie Thripp were sitting at a table writing prices on little slips of white paper.

"Bring those boxes over here," Mrs. Muckleroy said, "so we can price that merchandise."

Miss Mattie hurried up and started prowling through the first box.

"Oh, dear," she said, "what do you think we ought to charge for these toilet paper covers old Mrs. Bean crocheted?"

"Humph," Mrs. Muckleroy said, "we couldn't give those away. My Lord, who's got a bathroom done in orange and royal blue?"

"Or shocking pink and green!" Miss Mattie giggled.

"I thaw one in Juarez—" Miss Lonie said, looking up from the display of pot holders she was arranging.

Just then, Mrs. Crews walked up. "Lord love a duck!" she said, holding up a black and red one. "What is this?"

A crowd had begun to gather around the table.

"Well," Miss Julia Lockhart said, "ever since Mrs. Bean

came down with the Alzheimer's, she don't do a thing all day but crochet toilet paper covers. And since she can't drive, Mr. Bean buys all her yarn. He told me he just buys whatever's on sale."

"Let's just leave them in the box," Mrs. Muckleroy said. "She'll never know the difference."

"I don't think that would be right," someone said.

Just then, Butch came in wheeling a cart full of plants in plastic pots.

"Where do you want these?" he asked.

"Put um over here so we can put on the prices," Miss Mattie said.

Butch picked up one of the toilet paper covers and slid it over a flowerpot. It just fit.

"Oh, Butch. If you're not the thmartetht thing," Miss Lonie Fulkerson said. "Ithn't that cute?"

The women all oohed and ahhed over how smart Butch was and, pretty soon, they had set up a real colorful display of Butch's plants all dressed up in Mrs. Bean's crocheted covers.

By ten that morning, the Methodist fellowship hall looked like a department store. The tables were loaded with ornaments, Christmas tree skirts, wall hangings, and stockings. Miss Lonie's table where she displayed her ceramic Santa Claus heads and snowman cookie jars was next to Butch's display of decorated grapevine wreaths and fake flower arrangements sprinkled with glitter. Mrs. Muckleroy was guarding the table loaded with cakes and pies and Willie Mae's pecan pralines.

I was helping Mrs. Muckleroy with her display when

Mrs. Ben Birdsong walked in with her purse over her arm. She picked up one of the pies and smelled it.

"Who baked this?" she asked.

"I did," Mrs. Muckleroy said. "It's my sister's recipe for double chocolate bourbon pecan, but you can't buy it now. The bazaar doesn't start until one."

Mrs. Birdsong put both hands on her cheeks. "Oh, my gracious. I must have read the ad wrong. I could have sworn on a stack of Bibles the paper said ten."

Biggie walked up. "Is there a problem?" she asked.

Mrs. Birdsong fished down in her purse. "I cut the notice out. It's here somewhere." She pulled a clipping out of her purse and read, " 'Christmas Bazaar, sponsored by the Daughters of the Republic of Texas, James Royce Wooten Chapter, to be held at the Methodist fellowship hall, December nineteenth at one P.M.' Oh, foot! What was I thinking?"

Biggie patted her on the shoulder. "Don't worry, Laverne. Let's us just go back into the kitchen and have a cup of coffee. Then when the ladies are finished setting things up, you can be our first customer."

Mrs. Birdsong looked grateful and followed Biggie to the church kitchen. Biggie went over to the big silver urn and poured two cups of coffee in white mugs. She brought them to the kitchen table where Mrs. Birdsong had flopped down in a folding chair. She set her big black purse on the floor beside her.

"I declare, Ben's right," she said. "I ain't got the sense God promised a goose. I could've swore up and down the paper said ten."

Biggie took a swig of coffee and made a face. "Don't worry, honey," she said spooning sugar into her mug. "We haven't had time for a chat in I don't know how long. How's Ben holding up?"

"Oh, him. He's fine," Mrs. Birdsong said. "I swear, I think he's better'n he's been in a great long time." She lowered her voice. "Between you and me, Ben and Firman never got along too good. Now, Biggie, don't you tell that."

"I won't," Biggie said. "I have to admit, though, I'm surprised. Those two always seemed so close."

"Oh, close. Yeah, I guess. It's just that Firman was, well—honestly, Biggie, he like to drove Ben crazy sometimes with his sloppy ways. It was like he, I don't know, had somehow got out of step with the rest of the world."

"How so?"

Mrs. Birdsong leaned forward. "Now, Biggie, if you tell I said this, I'll say you lied, but remember the time Firman went off on that picture-taking trip of his?"

"Sure," Biggie said, "Ben told me all about it. I saw some real nice shots Firman had taken hanging in Ben's office."

"Well, I'll give him that. Firman could take pretty pictures." Mrs. Birdsong got up and refilled her mug. "It's just that, when he came back home off that trip, he'd changed. Hung up his camera and never taken it out of its case again."

"What's so crazy about that?" I asked. "Maybe he just got tired of taking pictures."

"I agree," Biggie said.

"Oh, that wasn't all by a country mile," Mrs. Ben said. "There was the way, like I said, his personality taken a change."

"You mean Fairy Lee?" I said. "I heard he was in love . . . Ouch!" Biggie had pinched me under the table.

Mrs. Birdsong stared at me, then shook her head. "Oh, no, that was nothing but idle talk. He never would've done . . ." She started in talking real fast. "I meant the way he let himself get fat as a pig and never took any notice of his appearance. You remember how he used to dress so nice? Well, before long he started looking like his clothes had been flung at him with a pitchfork." She grabbed her purse and stood up. "Fairy Lee wasn't anything more'n an employee, that's all. Biggie, do you suppose I could buy me that pie now?"

Biggie looked at the clock over the sink. "You bet, Laverne. And don't forget to look at our other fine merchandise, too." She stood up and guided Mrs. Ben toward the door. "By the way, honey, where did Firman live? I don't think I ever knew."

"He had him a little old dinky apartment fixed up on the top floor of the Fresh-as-a-Daisy building," she said. "I used to ask him all the time why he didn't get him a house. Lord knows, he could've afforded one. He'd just look at me and say, why should he have a house to worry with when he could be right there amongst his chickens. Chickens was his life, I guess."

"Has anybody been up to his apartment since he died?" Biggie asked. "To clean, or anything?"

"Nope," Mrs. Birdsong said, wiggling out of her coat. "I guess that'll be my job. My land, it's getting hot in here. Mind if I leave my coat in the kitchen?"

"It'll be fine," Biggie said. "Who has the key to the apartment?"

"Ben, I guess. I know I sure don't."

"Laverne, honey," Biggie said, "do me a favor and don't have that apartment cleaned until I can look it over. We may find a clue there that could lead us to Firman's killer."

Mrs. Birdsong began to edge toward the door. I could hear a lot of cackling in the hall that told me they'd opened the doors for customers to come in.

"I gotta go," she said. "I've got my eyes on those potted plants Butch brought with their colorful covers. I bet they'll sell real fast."

"What about the apartment?" Biggie asked.

"See Ben," she said over her shoulder. "I ain't going to have the time to mess with it until after the holidays."

I walked back out into the fellowship hall and found Rosebud stacking boxes behind a screen in the corner.

"You about as much help as a wart on a hog's tit," he said. "Where you been?"

"Busy helping Biggie interrogate a suspect. When can we go home?"

Rosebud dropped the box he was holding. "Now. I feel like beating you at a game of Chinese checkers before supper."

12

"How'd the bazaar come out, Miss Biggie?" Willie Mae asked the next morning.

"Best ever," Biggie said, standing on tiptoe to put the platter she'd just dried on the top shelf. "We sold everything but the cash box."

I was sitting at the kitchen table watching Rosebud build a house out of a deck of cards while Biggie and Willie Mae cleaned up the breakfast dishes.

"Don't put that up there," I said. "The whole thing's gonna fall."

"What are you talking about, J.R.?" Biggie said. "We always keep the platter up here."

"No, Biggie, the card house. Looky. It's nearly as tall as me."

"This ain't nothing," Rosebud said. "You ain't gonna

believe this, but once I built one as tall as that there refrig-erator."

"Uh-uh!" I said.

"If I'm lyin', I'm dyin'," Rosebud said. "It was down in Port Arthur. You remember, honey?"

Willie Mae walked over to the table and stared hard at the card house. I swear, she never touched that table, but I saw it with my own two eyes—that card house just began to come apart, one card at a time, real slow, 'til it wasn't a thing but a pile of bicycles scattered all over the top of Big-gie's kitchen table.

"Now, honey," Rosebud said.

"Git them cards off my table so I kin knead my bread."

"Never mind," Biggie said. "Rosebud, I want you to drive me out to Fresh-as-a-Daisy this morning. J.R., you can come along with us."

"Can I visit our Christmas turkey?" I asked.

"Sure."

"You want to see him, Rosebud?" I asked.

"Not me," Rosebud said. "I don't never eat nothin' once I've seen it walkin' around, and I plan on eatin' a goodly portion of that feller."

Biggie opened the back door and stepped out onto the porch. I followed her. Everything had turned brown, ex-cept for the big spruce tree in the side yard and the English ivy that grows up to the top of the chimney and then tum-bles back down over the roof. The wind was icy and smelled like burning leaves. Christmas weather.

"Biggie, do you reckon we'll have a white Christmas?" I asked.

Biggie put her hand on my shoulder. "I doubt it. We

hardly ever get snow until January, if then." She looked up at the sky. "Clouds are clearing. That means it'll be freezing cold today. Go bundle up. Wear your cap and gloves."

When we got to Fresh-as-a-Daisy, we found Ben Birdsong standing in the yard talking with one of his foremen. He was holding a clipboard with some pages of numbers.

"This here's the bottom line, Wendall," he asid. "You don't bring em in under this figure, we don't give out Christmas bonuses this year. It's all right here in black and white. Oh, er, Miss Biggie. Well, uh, what I mean to say is, how can I help you?"

"Could we go inside?" Biggie asked. "It's colder than an Eskimo's outhouse this morning."

"Can I see our turkey?" I asked.

Mr. Ben looked down at me like he'd just discovered I existed. "Oh, sure, I reckon so. It's in Barn Number Two. Wendall here will show you."

It was warm in the barn and smelled like feed and turkey manure, which smells a good bit like chicken manure. Wendall pointed out four cages that each held one turkey. The second cage had a sign on the front that said "Miss Biggie Weatherford." I walked over and peered in at the bird, who was stuffing himself with corn. He looked at me and let out a loud gobble. I turned and ran out of there, thinking Rosebud was right. It's not much fun to meet up with a critter when you know he's about to be your dinner. That might present a problem when I ran away to live off the land. I reckoned I might just have to live on fish, on account of it isn't too easy to get personal with a fish.

When I got back to the office building, Biggie and the others were sitting on leather chairs in the outer office and drinking coffee. Biggie was telling Ben about how she wanted to take a look at Firman's home.

"I wouldn't say it's what you'd exactly call a home," he said. "It's more like, well—you can see for yourself. Come this way."

Biggie set down her coffee cup, and we followed Ben down several halls, each getting narrower and darker as we went. Finally we came to some elevator doors. Ben pushed a button, and the doors creaked open.

"This is the only way to get there," he said. "Not many people even know this part of the building exists."

"Why so secret?" Biggie asked as the elevator rattled to a stop.

"Oh, it's no secret. It's just that this wing's not used anymore since we built the annex next door. Old Firman, he didn't much care where he bunked down. He said one place is just about as good as another." He pushed open a dirty green door. "Nothing's been moved," he said.

"I know," Biggie said. "Laverne told me she wouldn't get around to it until after the holidays. Now I see why."

Rosebud hadn't said much. Now he spoke up. "It ain't nothin' but a bachelor's pad. A man needs a woman to make a nice home. I seen a place worse than this once. It was . . ."

"Not now, Rosebud," Biggie said. "Let's start searching. Ben, you can go if you want. If we take anything away, I'll make a list for you."

Mr. Ben left, saying he did need to get back to his end-of-year accounting.

The room was real small and had a slanted ceiling owing to the fact that it was way up in the attic of the building. It had two little windows up near the roof. The only other light was the lamp on the nightstand beside the big king-sized bed, which was covered with a green velvet spread. Clothes and old magazines with pictures of chickens were thrown everywhere, on the floor, the bed, and covering the tops of all the furniture. Beside a big leather chair stood a coffee can with dried tobacco spit in it. The place was hot and musty smelling. Rosebud went to the windows and threw them open, letting in a blast of icy air.

Biggie told Rosebud to look through the dresser drawers while she tackled the closet. She had me go through the cedar chest at the foot of Mr. Birdsong's bed.

Rosebud started pawing through the dresser drawers, muttering to himself about how a man really needed a good woman. "Looky here," he said, holding up a pair of big ratty undershorts. "Holes all in um. Um-um. Ain't it a shame." He held up a brush so full of hairs you could hardly see the bristles. "No wonder his hair always looked like it'd been combed with a rake. Shoot, a rake would've done a better job."

Biggie was going through the clothes in his closet. "Well, he has some mighty fine suits here," she said, looking at the labels. "He must have worn these when he was out hobnobbing with the politicians in Austin."

I opened the cedar chest. It was full of blankets and sheets, not folded or anything, just stuffed in any old way. I closed the lid and walked over to the closet. Biggie was standing on tiptoe trying to look on the top shelf.

"Come here, Rosebud," she said. "I think I see a box way in the back."

Rosebud reached up with his big black hand and brought down a white box, the kind they put suits and dresses in at the store. He set it on the bed and took off the lid. It was filled with photographs and old letters.

"These must be the pictures Laverne spoke about." Biggie pulled out a handful and spread them across the bed.

I gotta admit, Mr. Firman Birdsong was a mighty good photographer—and you could tell he'd traveled all across the country. There were pictures of Maine lighthouses and Florida beaches, tall buildings in New York and Chicago, and neon signs in Las Vegas.

"Wow! Look at this." I held up a color shot of the Grand Canyon. "I want to go there!"

"You will, honey," Biggie promised.

"I recollect the time . . ." Rosebud said.

Biggie gave him a look, and he hushed. She was looking through some small snapshots of people. I peered over her shoulder. Most of them were girls. One was a redhead standing in the surf wearing a little bitty swimsuit; one was a brunette sitting on a horse; one was a blonde wearing nothing but a scarf.

When she saw me looking, Biggie stuffed those pictures back in the box and picked up a big one in a paper frame.

"What's that, Biggie?"

She was staring at the picture. It showed a young man and woman and a teenage boy sitting on a fence. They were dressed in jeans and boots and leather chaps. They all had on cowboy hats pushed back on their heads and were grinning like a tree full of possums. A sign behind them said,

MESQUITE RODEO, 1967. All three looked familiar, but I couldn't figure where I'd seen them.

Biggie turned the picture over and showed me what was written on the back: "Janie Pearl, Skinny, and me at the rodeo."

"Biggie!" I said.

Just then Rosebud, who had gotten tired of the photos and gone back to the dresser, let out a holler. "Whee-haw! We got him, now. Sure as snuff!"

Biggie put down the picture. "What?"

Rosebud held a crumpled piece of school notebook paper in front of Biggie's face. I could see that the words were printed with a lead pencil that could do with sharpening.

dear firman birdsong,

you are a ded man if you mess with my woman again. if you dont think i mean this well you just try. a man that will fool with another mans wife deserves to die. I dont care if you fire me or not.

watch out,
a desperit man

Biggie stared at the letter. "Well, shoot a bug," she said.

"Who you reckon wrote it, Biggie?" I asked.

"One Mr. W. C. Watkins is my guess."

"Who's that?"

She looked right through me.

"Biggie, who is W. C. Watkins?"

She shook her head. "Oh, that's Dub, of course. Dub is short for *W.*"

"What do you think, Miss Biggie?" Rosebud asked.

Biggie started putting the pictures back in the box. She folded the letter and stuck it in her purse. "I think it doesn't look good for Dub. Bring the box, Rosebud. We've got to get back to town and tell Paul and Silas to get a search warrant so we can take a look at the arsenal Fairy Lee says he's hidden out behind his house." She took a step toward the door and tripped, falling against Rosebud. "What was that? Oh, just a wrinkle in the rug. Let's get out of this messy place."

When the elevator creaked to a stop on the first floor, Mr. Ben was waiting for us.

"I was just about to go home for lunch," he said.

"It's okay, Ben," Biggie said. "We're through here. Mind if I take this box of pictures?"

"Keep um," Mr. Ben said. "I ain't got any use for them."

We found Paul and Silas sitting at the counter in the Owl Café having a plate lunch and talking to Mr. Populus about crime in Job's Crossing.

"The crimes, they are rampant," Mr. Populus said. "First there is the mayor dead in my good cake, next that undertaker, now Mr. Chicken Man. One more, and Populus will take his business to Center Point for sure!"

"You're right," Paul and Silas said. "I was safer associating with bikers and cutthroats than here in this sleepy little town."

"Horse patootie!" Biggie said, sliding onto a stool beside Paul and Silas. "You're as safe here as in your mother's arms. Now hurry up and eat. You have to get a warrant to search Dub Watkins's place. And while you're at it, you might as well get one for old Clovis Threadgill. We've got to get that gun of his one way or the other."

Paul and Silas looked sad. "Whatever you say, Cousin Biggie. I'll just finish my pie, and we'll be on our way."

13

The next morning when I woke up, the ground was covered with white. I jumped out of bed, pulled on my clothes, and hurried outside. But the white stuff wasn't snow. It was only sleet. Booger had followed me out and was walking on the grass, lifting his feet real high and shaking the sleet off with each step. I opened the door, and he shot back into the house like a six-legged jackrabbit.

When I came back in, I found Biggie peering out the den window. "Treacherous," she said. "I'll bet the streets are slick as watermelon seeds. Oh, well, we'll just have to walk."

"Walk where, Biggie?"

"Why, to town, of course. I haven't even started my Christmas shopping."

I love Job's Crossing at Christmastime. The decorations around the square are always real colorful, and the store windows are all fancied up with lights, tinsel, and greenery.

This year Butch had put a speaker in front of his shop so he could play Christmas music for everyone who passed down the street. "Santa, Baby" by Eartha Kitt was playing real loud when we got there. Cooter McNutt, dressed in a dirty old Santa suit, was standing beside a black pot in front of the police station. He was ringing a brass bell. His sign said, "Rotary Club Toys for Poor Kids." Biggie stepped up to him and dropped a dollar bill in his pot. Cooter pulled it out and examined it.

"Can't be too careful," he explained. "Lots of counterfeit money floatin' around at Christmastime."

"Merry Christmas, Cooter," Biggie said. "It's mighty nice to see you working for charity. I never would have thought it."

Cooter's shoulders slumped. "No'm," he said.

"Are you getting paid?" I asked.

Cooter sighed and put his hand on his hip. "No, that there Paul and Silas is makin' me do whatcha call 'community service.' I was plannin' to spend the season in a nice warm jail cell and have Mr. Populus's chicken and dressin' special for my dinner." He wiped away a tear with his grubby glove. "Now just look at me, standin' out here colder'n a possum in a deep freeze, ringin' this here goddamn bell!"

"Cheer up, Cooter, here's a little something just for you," Biggie said, stuffing some bills in his Santa suit pocket. Then she turned and went into the police station.

Paul and Silas was hanging up the phone when we got there.

"Cousin Biggie," he said, "I was just this very minute trying to call you. I've got good news and bad news."

"Well, spit it out," Biggie said, pouring herself a cup of coffee.

"First the good news. We've got more evidence against Dub. Want to hear it?"

"Paul and Silas, honey, for a Wooten, your brains often come loose and rattle around in your head. Of course I want to hear it."

Paul and Silas grinned. "You're right. If I was bright, I wouldn't be here. Anyway, Bertram Handy dropped by the station yesterday afternoon. He wanted to know how our investigation was going, and I told him not too good. Well, Bertram thought I ought to know that two days before he was killed, Firman was in Handy's House of Hardware purchasing rat poison."

"Well, I expect they use tons of that out at Fresh-as-a-Daisy," Biggie said, "what with all that chicken feed and all. Is that it?"

"No, there's more. Bertram went on to say that while he was measuring out the rat poison, who should walk in but Dub Watkins looking for a pair of jumper cables. He said old Firman turned white as a sheet when he saw Dub, and his hands started to shake so bad he could barely write out his check." Paul and Silas took a deep breath and continued. "When Dub saw Firman, he parked himself right by the door where Firman would have to pass him in order to leave—just stood there waiting, with his arms folded."

"Interesting," Biggie said, "but I wouldn't call that evidence."

"Cousin Biggie, I'm not finished yet," Paul and Silas said. "Bertram said that when Firman tried to leave, Dub grabbed him by the shirt collar and spoke to him very rudely, then shook him so hard Firman had to grab the doorjamb to keep from falling down."

Biggie nodded. "Interesting. What's the bad news?"

Paul and Silas got up from his desk and went to refill his coffee mug. "The bad news is, Judge Goolsby's out of town until after Christmas. He and Mrs. Goolsby went to Michigan to visit their daughter, Toots, and her family. That means I can't get that search warrant you wanted."

"How about Oprah Lee Simmons, the JP?" Biggie asked. "She can issue a warrant."

"Miss Oprah Lee's in the hospital over in Shreveport. She had to have her knee operated on."

"I told Oprah Lee she ought to lose some of that weight. Let me think a minute."

Biggie walked to the window and stared out at the square. I stood beside her and watched the people go by. Everyone seemed in a hurry—not a grouchy hurry, a happy, smiley-faced hurry. It made me feel good until I remembered I might not get to enjoy another Christmas in Job's Crossing.

Just then, Biggie spoke, still looking out the window. "Would you look at that? Meredith Michelle Muckleroy's got a new fake fur coat. I'll bet it's an early Christmas present. Ruby spoils that girl until it's pitiful."

Paul and Silas shook his head. "Cousin Biggie, is that all you've got to say? I thought we were working on a case here. What about Dub?"

"Oh, Dub." Biggie turned to face him, "Well, just go over to his house and arrest him for keeping gamecocks. Take Rosebud along with you in case you run into trouble. I know you can't keep him long, but it'll give us time to . . ."

119

"Don't tell me," Paul and Silas said. "What you're planning to do is illegal."

Biggie grinned. "Okay. Just have him in the pokey by four o'clock today. Come on, J.R., we've got shopping to do."

By the time we got home, I was worn out from carrying Biggie's packages. She'd bought a jogging suit for Rosebud, a fuzzy robe for Willie Mae, slippers to match, a bed jacket for her sister, Wynona, who lives in West Texas and is the sickly type, and a teapot shaped like a poodle for Mrs. Moody next door.

"Put all that stuff in my room," she said. "I'll start wrapping as soon as we get back from searching Dub's place."

The house was nice and warm and smelled like mincemeat pies. Rosebud had made a fire in the den and plugged in the Christmas tree lights. Biggie fell into her easy chair with a sigh.

"I just *love* Christmas," she said, then raised her voice. "Willie Mae, what's for lunch?"

Willie Mae came across the front hall to the den, pushing a tea cart. "Git you feets off the coffee table," she said to me. "We're eatin' in front of the fire."

Willie Mae spread a checkered cloth over the big coffee table and set steaming bowls of her secret recipe, super-hot four-alarm tortilla soup, in front of me and Biggie and Rosebud, who had just come stomping in from loading the woodbox. In the middle of the table, she set a basket of fried tortillas. Then she put down some little bowls of chopped onions, grated cheese, sour cream, and sliced avocados. She set a plate of brownies on the side table.

I ate two bowls, and Rosebud ate three. Biggie managed to polish off four, but she doesn't put any extra stuff in her soup. She says it's a crime to mess up Willie Mae's good soup with all that extra stuff. She leaned back in her chair and burped real loud, which, if I'd done that, I'd have been in big trouble.

"I need a nap," she said, then looked from me to Rosebud. "You two be ready at four to go search Dub's place. I've got a feeling we're within hollering distance of wrapping this case up."

It had started sleeting again when Rosebud came back from helping Paul and Silas corral old Dub. He walked to the fireplace and stood in front of it, clapping his hands together.

"All done?" Biggie asked.

"Slicker 'n owl spit," Rosebud said. "He come meek as a newborn colt. You 'bout ready to go search that junkyard of his?"

"Don't you want to warm yourself by the fire first?" Biggie asked. "Willie Mae has a fresh pot of coffee out in the kitchen."

"No'm," Rosebud said, "I believe I'd 'bout as soon get on with it. No tellin' how long Paul and Silas'll be able to keep him in the pokey. All he's gotta do is make bond, and his lawyer, old Joe Frank Swilley, was hightailin' it across the street from the courthouse when I left from there."

The blowing sleet felt like frozen BBs when we got out of the car in front of Dub's place. I ran around to the side of the house to see if that mean dog was still tied in the yard, but he was gone. The water in his bowl was frozen solid, and his collar and rope were still tied to the tree.

"Let's look around back first," Biggie said. "If we don't

121

find his guns in the shed, we'll just have to break into the house."

I thought of something. "What about the old man, Biggie?" I asked, but the wind must have blown my voice away. Biggie didn't answer, just hurried around the side of the house toward the shed out back. I followed but stopped at a bedroom window and looked inside. The old man was asleep on a cot with his back to the window. He was covered with a ratty old quilt.

Biggie and Rosebud were already rummaging around in the toolshed when I came in. Actually, Dub had some pretty neat stuff out there. I found an old slingshot made out of a tree branch that would have been perfectly good with new rubber. I was starting to put it in my pocket when Biggie caught me and made me put it back.

"That's not yours," she said. "Rosebud, come here and move this engine fan so I can look in this foot locker. Oh, fudge! It's locked."

"Lemme see," Rosebud said. "Well, this here's only a combination lock. Move over some and let me get in close."

Rosebud moved the engine fan onto the dirt floor and knelt down beside the trunk. He put his ear next to the lock and began turning the dial. Before you could say Jack Robinson, he had that trunk open and was feeling around inside. Me and Biggie looked over his shoulder. Whatever was in there was covered with an army blanket.

"Well, I'll be switched," Biggie said after Rosebud pushed the blanket aside.

"Grenades!" I said. "I seen them in a whole buncha war movies."

"Saw," Biggie said automatically, "you *saw* them. What's underneath, Rosebud?"

Rosebud moved the grenades carefully and pulled back the next layer of blanket. There, resting on the old green blanket, were guns—all kinds. Pistols mostly, but I saw a couple of shotguns and one rifle at the very bottom of the chest.

"Do you see a twenty-two revolver, Rosebud?" Biggie asked.

Rosebud shook his head and started covering up the guns. Next, he laid the grenades back, being careful to put them right where he'd found them. He closed the trunk.

"Looks like we been on a water haul, Miss Biggie," he said. "There ain't a twenty-two in there."

I'd been wandering around the shed looking at stuff while they talked. My foot hit something soft, and I bent down to see what it was. It wasn't anything but a dead rat, which is exactly what you'd expect to see in a place like that. Only this rat had a little round hole in its belly.

"Looky here," I said. "This rat looks like he's been shot."

Rosebud looked. "Well, for certain, he wasn't shot with one of them guns. Miss Biggie, we might better look around some more. I betcha that rat got shot with a twenty-two."

Biggie had moved to the workbench and was pawing through the stuff on top. "And here it is!" She held up a screwdriver stuck through the trigger guard of a little gun. "Wrap it in your handkerchief, Rosebud. My goodness, who'd have thought there would be so many twenty-two revolvers in Job's Crossing. And all connected in some way with Firman Birdsong."

"Can we go now?" I asked.

"Not yet," Biggie said. "I just want to . . ."

Just then, a sound came from behind the shed.

Grrrr.

I peeked through a crack between the boards, and what I saw made me sure the search was over. It was Dub's pit bull. He was looking right at me, and the hair on his back stood straight up. And this time he wasn't tied to any tree.

"Run!" I yelled, heading for the car like a turpentined cat, with Biggie and Rosebud right on my tail.

We made it to the car without a second to spare. As Rosebud started the motor and sped off, I looked back and saw that old devil dog standing at the very edge of the yard, tail straight up and teeth bared. He never barked once, just watched until we turned the corner at the end of the block.

Biggie patted her hair back in place. "Good job," she said, as if we all hadn't come close to being ripped apart. "Now we have two possible murder weapons. Drive by the police station, Rosebud. We'll just drop this gun off for Paul and Silas to send on to the ballistics lab in Dallas. Tomorrow we'll have to find a way to get Clovis Threadgill's gun away from him. That may be the hardest job of all."

14

Biggie was sitting at the kitchen table drinking coffee and reading Miss Julia's column aloud to Rosebud when I came down for breakfast the next morning.

"It says here that Ma Raley out at the nursing home is doing better," she said. "Julia writes that as of last Monday, she was sitting up in a chair and seemed like she knew everybody. Pass me some more coffee, J.R."

I poured more coffee in Biggie's mug and sat down to wait for my eggs. "Does it tell anything about the murder, Biggie?" I asked.

"Hmmm, let me see. Oh, it says here that Toots Goolsby had to go into the hospital in Tyler. She passed a kidney stone. The doctor told Forest, that's her husband, the thing was the size of a half-dollar. My gracious, that must have been like giving birth to a half-grown porcupine!"

"I say," Rosebud said.

"The murder, Biggie," I said.

"Oh, here it is. Julia writes that the undertaker over in Center Point had to cut Firman's left shoe off of him. Seems he had the gout real bad." She put down the paper and got up from the table. "Eat up, you two. We've got to get out to Clovis Threadgill's place. First, though, I think we'll stop by the farm. I want to check out the area where Buster got shot."

Willie Mae had just slid three eggs sunny side up on my plate along with a slab of toast made with homemade bread. I broke off a piece of toast and dipped it in one of my egg yolks. "Um-um, this is good," I said, licking my lips. I started reading the paper Biggie had left behind. "It says here Mr. and Mrs. Cozart went over to Center Point to eat at the Magic Wok and then had to take care of some business," I said.

Rosebud laughed without making any noise and slapped his knee. "Reckon they did," he said. "I've eaten at that place before."

"Huh?" I said.

"Eat up," Biggie said. "We leave in ten minutes."

Monica was helping her daddy feed the cows when we came bumping down the lane to the farmhouse. She was wearing an old army jacket and had a red stocking cap pulled down over her ears. She grinned like a jack-o'-lantern when she saw us.

"Hey, Miss Biggie. Hey, Rosebud. Hey, J.R.," she said. "What'chall doin' way out here?"

"Investigatin'," I said. "I don't have time to mess around. We're here on official business."

"Ooo-wee," Monica said. "I'm gonna investigate, too. Can I, Miss Biggie?"

"Sure, honey," Biggie said. "Coy, can you let us borrow Monica for a little while? We need her to drive us over to the far side of the pasture, the place where Buster got shot."

Mr. Sontag hitched up his pants and let go with one of his world-class feats of tobacco spitting. He shot a stream of juice a good five yards. It landed right next to Buster, who was taking a nap in the sun. Buster flicked his ear and went right on sleeping.

"Sure thing," Mr. Sontag said. "We're pert near through feedin'. Go on, hon. And you mind Miss Biggie. Hear?"

Monica didn't hear him on account of she was already backing the old farm truck out of the tractor shed.

Me and Rosebud had to ride in back on account of the truck's cab would hold only two people. We dern near got our brains shook loose, what with Monica driving like Mario Andretti over that bumpy old plowed field.

"This way," Monica said after she yanked up the parking brake and jumped out of the truck. She ran toward a line of trees.

"Well, I know it's this way," I said, panting behind her. "I can smell them eggs, can't I?"

I looked back to see that Biggie was walking slow with her eyes glued to the rocky ground. The grass was yellow and crackled under our feet. Every now and then, she would pick up something, examine it, then throw it back on the ground. Rosebud was doing the same thing. Suddenly he stopped next to a cottonwood tree.

"Looky here," he said. "I reckon this must be the place where the feller that shot Buster was hid out."

I started toward him, but he held up his hand to stop me. "Stay!" he said, like I was a dog or something. I stayed where I was and watched as he squatted down and slowly ran his hands over the mashed-down grass.

"Here 'tis." He held up something shiny.

Biggie walked over and took it out of his hand. "It's a casing, all right. Is it from a twenty-two?"

"Yep," Rosebud said.

"Biggie," I said, "Mr. Threadgill was the one shootin' at us, and he was over on his place. How come the shell is here?"

"Did you see him?" Biggie asked.

"Well, no. But we heard him as plain as day. Didn't we, Monica?"

"Yeah," Monica said. "He called us lily-livered varmints."

"Okay," Biggie said. "You two have a seat on the tailgate of the truck while Rosebud and I finish looking for clues."

After Biggie and Rosebud got through walking around looking at the ground and not finding any more clues, Biggie announced it was time to go have a word with Clovis. Monica said she guessed she'd pass on account of she had to help her daddy some more. I offered to stay and help just to be neighborly, but Biggie made me go with her and Rosebud.

Mr. Threadgill's little white house looked lonely somehow, sitting so far down his red gravel driveway. There was a rickety lean-to next to the house where his old John Deere was parked. In back, I could see what must have been a garden plot once upon a time, but now the chicken-wire

128

fence was falling down, and dead weeds stood waist-high. Next to that was an old tin privy with the door standing half open. It looked like a good wind would topple it in no time flat. I hung back while Biggie and Rosebud walked up and knocked on the door of the house.

"Clovis!" Biggie called. "Clovis, are you in there?"

There was no sound but a rooster crowing somewhere.

"He can't be far off, Miss Biggie," Rosebud said, "or he'd've taken his mower."

Biggie called again, and Rosebud stepped up and pounded on the door. I was still hanging back a safe distance. I remembered how they'd said he'd gotten his hands on a real gun.

Biggie put her hand up and pushed the door.

Just then, I heard a loud cracking noise. "Biggie, watch out!" I hollered.

"Oh, bother," Biggie said, "that's nothing but the wind blowing that old tin privy. Now get on up here!"

I got up there because I'm more scared of Biggie when she's riled than any old Clovis Threadgill.

Biggie pushed the door open a little way. It was pretty near dark in there, but the light shining in through the torn window shades showed the shape of an old recliner sitting in front of what looked like an almost new television set. Biggie reached up and flipped on the lights, and just as she did, something bigger than a rat, and gray, scuttled out from under the chair and off toward the back of the house.

Rosebud pushed his hat back and scratched his forehead. "Gawd dawg," he said, "a derned possum."

Biggie was already making her way past stacks of old newspapers and piles of raggedy clothes toward the back room. Me and Rosebud followed. Just then, a weak, trembly voice came from the back of the house.

"Did you bring the sawbones?"

Biggie pushed open another door, and there, lying on a dirty old mattress on the floor, was old Clovis. And all around him was a big brown bloodstain. A gas heater stood next to the wall, showing orange flames behind the elements.

Biggie turned to Rosebud. "Drive back to the farm and call for the ambulance and then come right back here." She knelt down beside Clovis. "What happened, honey?" she asked.

"Dryer'n a dust devil," he rasped.

"What?"

Real slow, he moved his horny old finger to point toward his mouth.

"Oh," Biggie said. "J.R., go in the kitchen and bring back a glass of water."

"Me?" I said. "Biggie, there's a—"

"James Royce Weatherford, go in that kitchen and get this poor old man a drink of water! Get!"

I got.

There was no sink in the kitchen. Over by the back door, I saw a table with a wash pan and a bucket. I looked in the bucket and found water, but that's not all I found. Three june bugs and a daddy longlegs were floating on top. I looked around for a glass, but all I saw was a moldy old pie with one piece out of it on the kitchen table. Then I thought of something. The old man must have a well out back. Sure enough, right by the back porch was an old concrete well with a bucket hanging from a pulley. Nailed to a post, I found a gourd dipper. I dropped the bucket down the well until I heard a splash and then pulled it back up. The water was kind of green, but it smelled okay. I filled the dipper and took it back to Biggie. She was kneeling on the floor, holding the old man's hand.

"Here's your water, honey," she said. "Can you hold your head up?"

He moaned a good bit but finally raised up enough to reach the dipper. After he'd had a drink, he sank back down on the bed with a raspy sigh.

Biggie leaned forward and unbuttoned his shirt, then examined his chest. "J.R.," she said, "go back to the well and bring some clean water. Find a clean rag, too, if you can."

I found some ratty old underwear hanging on a line on the porch. I filled the washbasin with water and took down a pair of shorts for a rag. When I got back, Biggie was bending over Mr. Threadgill.

"Go out and watch for Rosebud," she said, "while I do what I can to clean him up. My stars! He's been shot three times!"

I was glad to go outside. It was hot in that house and smelled awful, I guessed from all that blood. I looked down the road for Rosebud, but all I saw was a farmer driving his tractor. Then I heard a rustling noise. It seemed to come from under the house. Squatting down, I peered around one of the concrete piers that held the house up off the ground. Something moved, but I couldn't tell what it was. I kept looking and, when my eyes adjusted to the darkness,

I saw six little yellow eyes staring back at me. I chucked a rock at whatever it was. The next thing I knew, I was being run over by a family of armadillos who must have been taking their naps under Mr. Threadgill's house. I stood up and brushed myself off as the critters went shuttling around the side of the house like three little army tanks. I looked around, this time hoping Rosebud wasn't coming on account of he would have laughed his head off if he'd seen what just happened. While I was brushing my pants legs, my eye fell on something almost buried in the dust. I picked it up and saw that it was old man Threadgill's holster. Then I heard Biggie's car turn into the drive. I ran out to meet Rosebud, holding up the holster, but he brushed past me and went straight to the bedroom.

"The ambulance oughtta be here any minute," he said, "seein' as how they was already out this way bringin' Miz Goolsby home from the hospital." Biggie had left Mr. Threadgill's shirt open, and with all the blood gone, I could see three small holes in him, one in his shoulder, one in his side, and one just to the right of his belly button. Biggie was wiping his face with the cold water.

"He's lost an awful lot of blood," she whispered, then leaned down and spoke to the old man. "Who did this to you, Clovis?"

He was mumbling something, but I couldn't hear what he said.

"Clovis," Biggie said, louder, "who shot you?"

Suddenly, the old man sat straight up in bed and in a loud voice said, "Birdsong done it!"

I like to jumped out of my skin. Then I looked at him

and saw he'd fallen back on the bed and was lying there with his mouth open and his eyes wide, staring at the ceiling. Biggie touched his neck for a minute, then closed his eyes and gently pulled the quilt over his face.

15

I sat on the edge of a wooden kitchen chair waiting for the ambulance to come. Biggie was, naturally, poking around the little house looking for clues.

"My soul," she said as she opened one of the kitchen cabinets, "there's not a scrap of food in the whole house. Whoever knew the poor old thing was living like this?"

"I reckon he mostly ate at the café," Rosebud said. "Populus gave him most anything he wanted free."

"Somebody must've baked him a pie," I said.

"What?"

"On the table. There's a piece missing, Biggie."

Biggie picked up the pie and smelled it. "Dewberry. About a week old, I'd say."

"Reckon you might ought to see if you can't find out who brought that pie," Rosebud said.

"Yeah," I said. "It might be poisoned!"

"Who said?" Rosebud asked.

"Huh?"

"How come you say this pie might be poisoned when this here old man been shot?"

"Well—" I said. "Oh, I know! See, somebody got mad at Mr. Threadgill on account of he's—was—always going around talking mean to people and pointing his gun at them, so whoever it was baked him a poison pie. Then the person came back a few days later to see if he was dead, and he wasn't on account of he must've tasted the poison and decided not to eat any. See? So the person just went ahead and shot him. Get it?"

Biggie gave me a look, then picked up the pie and looked at the bottom of the glass pie plate. I could see a piece of tape stuck to the bottom, which is what ladies do when they want to put their names on the dishes they take to church suppers and funerals and stuff so the other ladies won't carry them off.

"I can see some writing," she said, "but it's all smeared."

"Let me look," Rosebud said. He took the pie to the window where the light was good. "Can't nobody read this. Ain't nothing but an ink smear on here."

Biggie found a grocery sack on the floor. "Slide the pie in this. I'll look at it with my magnifying glass at home."

I wandered into the front room, thinking I might watch a little TV while we waited. I sat down in the old man's recliner and dug around looking for his remote. It wasn't in the seat, so I reached my hand under the chair thinking it might be there. I felt something, but I could just reach it with the tips of my fingers. Whatever it was kept sliding farther away when I touched it, so I got down on all fours and looked underneath the chair. What I found amid all the dust bunnies and dead roaches wasn't the remote. It was Mr. Threadgill's gun.

"Biggeee!" I yelled.

"Don't touch it," Biggie said, coming into the room. She bent over and examined the gun as it lay on the floor. "Rosebud, do you have a handkerchief?"

Rosebud pulled a square of black silk out of his pocket.

"Ah-umm," I said, "Willie Mae's gonna get you. That's one of her special scarves she conjures with."

Rosebud just grinned and picked up the gun with the scarf. He released the cylinder and dropped three shells in his hand, then wrapped the gun and slid it and the bullets into his pocket.

"Ambulance!" I yelled, running for the front door. Sure enough, the ambulance came bouncing down the driveway with the siren going full blast. Butch jumped out the passenger side, and Fire Chief Frobisher climbed from behind the wheel.

Biggie put her hands over her ears. "Turn that thing off. We have a dead man here."

"Ooh, yuck!" Butch said, opening the rear door and pulling a gurney out. "Well, I'm not looking at him until after the undertaker's through."

Biggie led them to the bedroom. I hung around out back while they loaded him into the ambulance. When I heard it drive away, I started toward our car, hoping it was time to go.

Biggie was already in the passenger seat, and Rosebud had started the motor. As the car was turning out of the driveway, a rusty old Fordson tractor came creeping down the road. The oldest and blackest man I'd ever seen was driving it.

"Stop him," Biggie said to Rosebud. "That's E. C. Isom. He owns the twenty-five-acre tract just north of here. Let's ask him if he's seen or heard anything."

Rosebud pulled the car over, got out, and stood in the middle of the road so the tractor had to stop or run over him. He motioned the driver to pull over to the shoulder.

"Hidy, Mr. Isom," Biggie said, shading her eyes from the sun as she looked up at him. "I'm Biggie Weatherford from town. You used to sell fresh vegetables to my mama off the back of your wagon during the war. I was Fiona Wooten. Remember?"

The old man smiled. "Sho is! You ain't growed much."

"And your wife, Maymee, used to iron for us. How's she doing?"

"Fine, fine," he said, " 'cept when her arthuritis act up."

"Ya'll still got your farm?"

"Yes'm."

"I remember you used to grow the best roasting ears in the county."

"Yes'm."

"You can't get good roasting ears like that anymore."

"I know that's true."

I wished she'd get on with her questions so I could get home in time to watch *Unsolved Mysteries,* but I wasn't counting on it. I've known Biggie long enough to know there's no rushing her.

"How well did you know your neighbor, Clovis Threadgill?" Biggie asked.

"Not too good."

"Did you ever see anybody come visiting here?"

"No'm." The old man took off his straw hat and scratched his gray head. "Not before last Saturday."

"You saw someone last Saturday?"

"Yes'm. Sho' did."

"Could you tell us who it was?"

"No'm. I couldn't see who it was. But they run over my wife's puppy. She was right fond of that puppy."

"What a shame!"

"I know that's right."

"Did you see the car?"

"Yes'm, I seen it. A big old black one. Puts me in mind of this here one." He pointed to Biggie's car. "They didn't even slow down when they hit my wife's puppy."

"Well, thanks, Mr. Isom," Biggie said. "You've been a big help. Oh, I should tell you, Clovis Threadgill has been killed. Somebody shot him."

"My oh my. Do tell."

"I'd advise you and Maymee to be extra careful out here all alone."

"Yes'm. We sure will do that."

"And, if you think of anything else that might help us find the person who killed Maymee's puppy, just call up the police station. Will you?"

The old man nodded and gave a little wave as he put his tractor in gear and rumbled off down the road.

That night after supper, me and Rosebud sat on the floor in front of the fireplace playing a game of Scrabble while Biggie looked over Mr. Firman's box of pictures.

"Rosebud," I said, "*flodo* is not a word!"

Rosebud grinned, showing the gold hearts, clubs, diamonds, and spades in his front teeth. "I reckon they don't teach you everything over at that schoolhouse."

I stood up. "I'm getting the dictionary."

"Ain't everything in the dictionary," Rosebud said. "Go get me a cup of coffee, and I'll prove to you *flodo* is a word. If I can use it in a sentence, will you believe me?"

"Well . . ."

"Then go on and get my coffee."

When I got back with the coffee, Rosebud had pushed the Scrabble board out of the way and was sitting cross-legged, staring into the fire.

"It happened in the olden times, in a place called Storyville. I wasn't born yet, but my grandpa told it to me—and he was there, doncha know."

I took one of Biggie's needlepoint cushions off the sofa and lay down by the fire.

"I bet there ain't such a place as Storyville," I said. "I bet you just made that up. Right, Biggie?"

"What?" she said. Biggie was slumped down in her chair, looking at Mr. Firman's snapshots with her magnifying glass.

"Storyville," I said. "That's just a made-up name, ain't it, Biggie?"

"*Isn't*," she said. "How many times do I have to remind you not to say 'ain't'? No, Storyville isn't made up; it's a section of New Orleans—or used to be." Suddenly she sat up straight. "Rosebud, what are you telling this boy?"

Rosebud winked at her. "Nothin' he shouldn't hear. So, anyway, Mr. Smarty, my grandpa used to be sweet on a cute little Creole gal name of Thea LaRusse what lived with her ma in a place called Storyville. Every Saturday night he'd call on her at her mama's place of business, La Jardin des Fleurs, where Thea played the piano for some high-falutin' white fellers who used to drop in from time to time to visit with her mama and her sisters."

I yawned. "Rosebud, what's this got to do with *flodo*?"

"Ain't I gettin' to that?" Rosebud said. "If folks would just hush and give a feller a chance. See, what happened was, one of these white boys got his feelin's awful hurt on account of one of Thea's sisters wouldn't have nothin' to do with him because he came callin' straight from his shrimp boat. He wouldn't take a bath or nothin'. Well, if you ain't never smelled day-old shrimp juice on a feller's clothes . . ."

"So, what'd he do?"

"Wellsir, not only was that feller unsanitary, so to speak, he was a sneak and a liar. What he done was, he went to see his brother-in-law who was a police officer and told him that Thea's mama and her sisters was . . ."

"Rosebud!" Biggie said.

". . . was selling pecan pralines without a license, which was against the Napoleonic Code, doncha know."

"The what?"

"The law, son, the law. Well, anyway, after that, the cops would raid Miz LaRusse's parties just about every other Saturday night and confiscate all her pralines, you see. Well, I don't have to tell you, Miz LaRusse got mighty tired of that, so she commenced lookin' around for a way to hide the candy so they'd never find it."

"What'd she do?" I asked, interested in spite of myself.

"Well, what she done was, she got a carpenter to come

and cut out a hole under the carpet with stairs goin' down to the cellar. Then, doncha see, every time they'd hear them heavy-footed cops comin', Thea and her mama and sisters would take all the candy and escape through the *flodo!*"

I picked up the Scrabble board and dumped all the tiles in the box. "I'm going to bed," I said.

Biggie was looking at Rosebud with a strange expression on her face. Then she smiled a slow smile. "Rosebud," she said, "I could kiss you."

"Why, Biggie?" I asked. "That story didn't make a bit of sense. Anyway, he just made it up to cheat at Scrabble."

"He pointed out something to me—even if he doesn't know he did it!"

I frowned at Rosebud, who was laughing his head off and not making a sound.

"You'll find out tomorrow," Biggie said. "Come give me a hug, then off to bed."

As I hugged Biggie, I noticed she was holding a picture of a black-haired girl smiling into the camera and sitting on a spotted pony.

16

The next morning, I slept late. When I got up, the sun was already high over Mrs. Moody's roof, and the sky was blue as Biggie's eyes. I pulled on my Dallas Cowboys sweatshirt and rooted around in my closet until I found my skateboard, thinking I might just go over to the loading dock back of the post office and practice a few jumps. When I came down for breakfast, Biggie had other ideas.

"Get your jacket and cap," she said. "We're going back out to Fresh-as-a-Daisy."

I decided I could skateboard later. "Cool," I said. "I want to see if our turkey's got any fatter."

"Set down and eat," Willie Mae said. "You ain't got enough meat on you to feed a sparrow."

"I'm little, but I'm fast," I said. But I sat down and waited until Willie Mae put a plate of scrambled eggs and bacon in front of me.

Rosebud came in the back door slapping his hands together. He rumpled my hair. "How 'bout another game of Scrabble?" he said, grinning.

"*Flodo's* not a word," I said. "You cheat." I turned to Biggie. "Do you reckon that person that ran over Miz Isom's puppy killed Mr. Threadgill?"

"Maybe, maybe not." Biggie got up and took a yellow tablet and a pen off the counter by the telephone. "Let's make a list of all the people we know who drive big black cars."

"I know one," Rosebud said, "Reverend Johnson at St. Thelma's CME. The church gave it to him with money left over from the new Sunday school building."

"And Mr. Plumley at the drugstore," I said. "He just bought a brand-new Buick. Oh, and Mrs. Muckleroy. She just had to have one just like yours. Remember, Biggie?"

"I remember," Biggie said, "but I was thinking of someone more . . . oh, well, I'll just have to check with all those people." She tore the page she'd been writing on off the pad and stuffed it in her purse. "Go brush your teeth," she said, "and we'll be off."

"Mrs. Muckleroy was at the café that night," I said. "Might be she killed Mr. Firman and Mr. Threadgill."

"Ruby Muckleroy can be a royal pain in the patootie," Biggie said, "but somehow I don't see her as a murderer." She stood up and started wiggling into her red-and-black hunting jacket. "Let's go or we'll be past lunchtime getting back."

Rosebud drove us out to the chicken plant, where we all decided to visit our turkey. He was tall, and his white feathers were shiny and clean. When he saw us, he gobbled real loud. I stuck my finger in his cage, and he came over and pecked me easy. Then he cocked his head and looked at me like he wanted to say something. I got out of there—fast. Rosebud was right. It's not good to get personal with something you plan on making a meal of later.

Mr. Ben looked put out when Biggie asked to be let into Mr. Firman's apartment again. He unlocked the door and walked away, muttering to himself about year-end bookkeeping.

The place was the same as we'd left it, only it smelled a good bit mustier, I guessed from all the dirty clothes being closed up in there so long. Biggie walked straight to the place where she'd tripped on the rug and poked it with her toe.

"Rosebud, can you move this rug out of the way?" she asked.

"Corner's under the bed," he said. "Come here, son. You pull the rug out while I heft her up." He grunted as he lifted the big bed. "Hurry now. I can't hold this thing while you be fiddlin' around."

The old rug was stuck to the floor, but I dug in with my fingernails and yanked it out just as Rosebud dropped the bed with a thud. He grabbed the rug and peeled it back to where Biggie was standing.

"Just as I thought." Biggie looked down at the floor. "A trapdoor!"

I looked, and sure enough, I could see where the boards were cut in a neat little square. Rosebud slid his knife into one of the cuts and gently raised it away from the rest of the floor.

"Well, whatcha know," he said. "A *flodo*!"

144

Biggie was already pawing through the space under the floor. She pulled out a packet of papers jammed into a plastic grocery sack.

"Come on," she said, stuffing the sack into her big black purse. "We'll look these over at home. I want to stop by the Piggly Wiggly and pick up some pork chops for supper."

After lunch, I took my skateboard down to the post office for some practice, but the wind just went right through me, so I gave up and came home. Miss Mattie, Butch, Mrs. Moody, and Miss Julia Lockhart were having coffee and fruitcake with Biggie in the parlor. I decided to sit on the stairs and eavesdrop since there was nothing better to do. They were discussing the Christmas yard display contest.

"Ruby Muckleroy thinks she's going to win again this year," Miss Julia said, "just because she's got two goats staked to the ground right next to her nativity scene. Claims that makes hers a living tableau. Course the Baby Jesus is Meredith Michelle's old Cabbage Patch doll."

"I heard they ate all the berries off her nandina," Butch said.

"I don't believe they had goats at the first Christmas," Miss Mattie said. "Just sheep and cows and a donkey."

"And camels," said Mrs. Moody. "Remember the wise men?"

"That was on Epiphany," Biggie said. "Twelve days later."

"Not in our church, it wasn't," Mrs. Moody said. "In our church they came on Christmas Eve just like the shepherds and the angels on high."

"Well, personally, I don't think she'll win," Butch said. "Especially if she can't keep Cooter McNutt from hanging around that nanny. I heard Royce Muckleroy had to turn the hose on him night before last."

I heard one of the ladies gasp.

"More coffee, Mattie?" Biggie said real fast.

"Just a tad," Miss Mattie said, "or I'll be up half the night.

"Well, I know I won't win," Miss Mattie went on. "Norman just insisted on putting carolers on the roof, and before I could stop him, he'd painted Masonic aprons on all of them. You know, Norman's real serious about his Masonry."

"What's wrong with that?" Mrs. Moody asked. "The Masons believe in Jesus, don't they?"

"Some do, but not all," Miss Julia said. "I know a lot about lodges. My first husband was a Knight of Columbus, but my third was an Elk. My daddy, he was a Moose. . . ."

"I think the Culver house on Oak Lane looks real nice," Butch said. "They've got that big yellow cat from the funnies dressed in a Santa suit and climbing down the chimney. Why don't you ever decorate, Biggie? You've just got the perfect house for it."

"A wreath on the door's good enough for me," Biggie said, picking up the cake plate. "I'll get some more cake from the kitchen."

I peered through the transom just in time to see Miss Mattie lean in toward the others.

"Ya'll be real nice to Biggie," she said. "She's bound to be worried sick about J.R."

"Really?"

"How come?"

"Tell, Mattie!"

Miss Mattie lowered her voice, and I scrunched in closer to the door.

"You know those Culpeppers?"

"Who doesn't?" Butch said.

"Well, that woman is J.R.'s other grandmother—and she's got a piece of paper saying she can take the boy anytime she gets good and ready. . . ."

I ran up to my room and didn't come down until suppertime. When I did come down on account of I smelled pork chops cooking, Biggie had all the papers she'd found in Firman's apartment spread over the dining room table. She was grinning like a possum eating persimmons and even did a little dance step as she went in to sit down at the kitchen table.

"You mighty happy tonight," Willie Mae said, looking hard at Biggie.

"I should be," Biggie said. "All my problems are solved."

I felt a lump in my throat. How could Biggie say that?

"You mean 'cause of them papers ya'll brought home?" Willie Mae asked.

"That's right," Biggie said. "Pass me the gravy."

"Don't be so sure," Willie Mae said. "Most times, the easy answer ain't always the right answer."

"Now, honey," Rosebud said. "I read them papers. . . ."

Willie Mae shook her finger at Rosebud. "I know what I know. And this family ain't out of the woods yet. Miss Biggie, you be careful, you hear?" She got up, cut a big piece of lemon icebox pie, set it in front of me, and laid her hand on my head. It made me feel tingly all over.

"How 'bout a game of Scrabble?" Rosebud said with a twinkle.

"I'm goin' up to my room," I said.

When Biggie came up to say good night, I was counting my money again. I stuffed it back in the sack and pushed it under my pillow.

"You okay?" she asked, taking a seat on my bed. "You seem upset."

"It's—uh—it's Rosebud. Why does he have to cheat, anyway? Biggie, you reckon he thinks I don't know *flodo's* not a word?"

"Of course not, J.R. He's just teasing you."

"Well, what's it supposed to mean?"

"It's old-timey country talk, J.R. It means floor-door."

"Oh."

"Do you remember what tomorrow is?" Biggie asked.

"No'm."

"It's Christmas caroling on the square. You always have fun at that. There'll be hot cider and roasted peanuts, and the Methodist choir will be dressed up in Victorian clothes. After the singing, the mayor will name the winner of the best-decorated house."

I sat up straight in bed. "Biggie, I just thought of something. You know how Monica never has any fun on account of being stuck out in the country all the time?"

"What are you talking about, J.R.? Monica has more fun than anybody I know."

"I mean *town* fun, Biggie. How about if we ask her to come spend the night tomorrow night? She can go with us. I bet she'd just love to hear the carols and stuff."

Biggie gave me a suspicious look. "What are you up to, J.R.?"

"Nothing, really, Biggie. I just want to do a good turn 'cause it's Christmas and all."

"I suppose so, then," Biggie said, giving me a kiss on the cheek. "Now you sleep well and wake up in a better mood tomorrow."

"Yes'm."

I knew it was time to put my plan in motion before those Culpeppers got their hands on me. But I needed Monica's help to make it work.

17

The courthouse square in Job's Crossing is always a sight for sore eyes at Christmastime. People from as far away as Mount. Pleasant drive over every night during the season just to get a look at it. The firemen string white lights all over the big square courthouse and around the pecan trees on the lawn. This year, they even covered the statue of old James Royce Wooten, Biggie's ancestor who guards the square, with lights. The little white bandstand with the gingerbread trim, where the Methodists were belting out "Oh Little Town of Bethlehem," glowed like a birthday cake. Rosebud pulled the car into a parking space in front of the Owl Café.

"Ooo-wee," Monica said, hopping out the back door, "I smell parched peanuts." She ran across the street to a stand Roy Lee Peoples from the Eazee Freeze had put up. The sign said: HOT ROASTED PEANUTS—$1 A BAG.

"Meet me back at the car at ten," Biggie said to me. "I'll

be at the bandstand listening to the program. Rosebud, get those lawn chairs out of the back and set them up as close as you can to the gazebo. J.R., you stay with Monica. She gets so excited when she comes to town, she's liable to do anything!"

"I ain't paying no dollar for a bag of peanuts," Monica was telling Roy Lee. "We got a whole peanut patch out at our farm."

"Okey-doke," Mr. Peoples said. "How 'bout a sodie water? I got Big Reds for a buck apiece."

"I can get one for half that at the Wag-n-Bag," Monica said. "Take my advice and drop your prices, or you might just as well go on home."

Mr. Peoples pulled a cigar box out from under his counter and opened it up. It was brimful of money. "It's the holiday spirit," he said. "Folks just love to spend money at Christmastime."

"Humph," Monica said. "Come on, J.R. Let's see what Butch is selling at his stand."

Butch had a stand draped all over with red and green streamers. He was dressed as an elf. "Get your figgy pudding," he said as we strolled over. "Gen-u-wine figgy pudding just like in the song."

"Lemme see some," Monica said.

Butch pulled a tray out from under the counter. It was covered with little squares of something that looked like cake set on paper doilies. Monica poked a finger toward the tray.

"No touching," Butch said. "Your finger's probably got germs on it."

"Well, what is it?" Monica wanted to know.

Butch put his hand on his hip. "Well, it's figgy pudding. Didn't you read the sign?"

"I mean, what in blue blazes is figgy pudding?" Monica put her nose down and sniffed one of the squares before Butch could stop her. "It smells like plain old gingerbread to me."

"Never mind." Butch pulled down a red shade to cover his booth and stepped outside. "They're about to announce the house-decorating winners, and I don't want to miss that. Ya'll want to come?"

We followed Butch over to the gazebo and found Biggie sitting next to Mrs. Ben Birdsong. Mrs. Birdsong looked sad.

"I just don't know what I'm going to do," she said. "Ben says Fresh-as-a-Daisy's not near as prosperous as he thought it was. I ought not to be telling you this. . . ."

Biggie patted her hand. "You don't have to worry about me. My mouth's shut tighter than a coffin."

"Well"—Mrs. Ben leaned closer so I had to strain to hear—"Ben *says* that Firman had gone and run up a lot of bills Ben didn't know about. But what I think is, I think Ben's just tighter than wallpaper, and he doesn't like me spending money." She patted the shopping bags on the ground beside her chair. "I tell you, Biggie, that old skinflint's not about to clip my wings. Not after I put up with . . ."

Just then the high school band started playing a loud flourish, and our new mayor stepped up to the podium. He adjusted the microphone, and it made a loud whistling noise.

Monica clapped her hands over her ears. "Gawd dawg!" she hollered.

"Shhh," I said.

"Ladies and gents," said Mayor Ballinger, "as your new mayor, it is my great privilege to announce the winners of this year's house-decorating contest. But first, let me say . . ."

"His mouth's so big it looks like a torn pocket," Monica said. "Looky there—how his lips just flop all over the place."

I put my hands over my mouth to stop a giggle.

". . . have instituted a fund-raising campaign to build a brand-new city jail, to replace the old relic we now have, which was built in nineteen-ought-four. Now, I have talked with an engineering firm from Dallas about this, and they say they can raze the old jail and build a brand-new one out of cement blocks for a mere one hundred and ninety thousand dollars."

Before a cat could lick his fanny, Biggie was on her feet. "Mr. Mayor," she said, but the mayor couldn't see her on account of her being so short.

"We'll have five state-of-the-art modern cells," he said, "and a drunk tank just like the one they have in San Antonio!"

"Mr. Mayor!" Biggie said. "Rosebud, lift me up so that peckerwood can see me."

Rosebud hoisted Biggie up on his shoulders. Now she had everyone's attention.

"Mr. Mayor," she said, "that jail is a historic building. Why, we once had the whole entire Light Crust Doughboys band locked up in there."

Mr. Handy, who owns Handy's House of Hardware, stood up. "I remember," he said. "That was when W. Lee O'Daniels was running for governor. Their driver got

153

drunk and drove their flatbed truck across Eddie Poole's rose garden. After that, a fight busted out, and they and a good number of our local citizens got locked up."

Mr. Plumley stood up. "That's right," he said. "I was just a boy, but I'll never forget that day. The sheriff made them play an entire concert in the park before he let them go. I can still see my mama wiping away a tear when they played 'Rosetta.' "

After that, a lot of other people stood up and shared stories about the old jail, until finally the mayor banged his gavel and promised to hold a town meeting to discuss the matter.

"Now," he said, "with your permission, I will announce the winners of the contest, starting with the prize for originality, which goes to the Muckleroy home. Let's give a big hand to Ruby Muckleroy and her goats!"

Mrs. Muckleroy walked up the steps to the gazebo. She was wearing a fur coat with a hat to match.

"My sakes," Mrs. Ben whispered, "that must have cost a pretty penny!"

The mayor awarded prizes for the cleverest decoration, the most lights, the best religious theme, and just as he was about to announce the winner of the best in humor, Monica stood up.

"This is boring," she said. "I know! Let's go talk to Willie Mae. Maybe she'll let us watch her conjure."

I asked Biggie, and she said okay, but only if we stayed on the sidewalk and went straight home. When we got to the house, Willie Mae was watching *Melrose Place* on the TV in the den. She turned off the set real fast and asked if we were hungry.

"I know I am," Monica said. "Those peckerwoods downtown will rob you blind if you let um. Course, I'm too smart to throw my money away. . . ."

Willie Mae whipped up a batch of cocoa and brought out some sugar cookies she'd made. Then she said she was going to bed and for us to be sure and put our dishes in the sink. I was glad to see her go on account of I needed to lay out my plan for Monica.

I told her all about the Culpeppers and how they wanted to take me away and how Biggie didn't seem to be doing anything to stop them.

"It's time for me to take matters in my own hands," I said.

"I reckon," Monica said, taking a bite of cookie. "What you gonna do?"

I told her about how I had better than ninety dollars saved up and how I thought I could live out at Betty Jo Darling's cabin until the Culpeppers gave up and went on back to Montana.

"Hmm," Monica said. "Might work. How you gonna eat?"

"I'll live off the land. Berries, nuts, wild grapes. I thought I could catch me a few fish, shoot a few squirrels."

"And I could steal stuff out of Mama's garden and milk from old Bess. Hey, this might be fun!"

"It's not a game. I'm fighting for my life here. Those Culpeppers might even be murderers."

"If they're murderers, Miss Biggie will find out and send them to jail. Then your troubles will be over."

I didn't answer that. I was too busy plotting my getaway. "Here's the problem," I said. "I'm going to need some stuff from home, like my fishing pole and my daddy's rifle, but my only transportation is my new bike. Got any suggestions?"

"Yep. First of all, you don't need your pole. You can cut one from a willow tree down by the creek. Just bring along some hooks and line. As for your gun, tell Miss Biggie you're loaning it to me, and I'll take it home tomorrow. We can cram a lot of clothes and stuff into in my overnight bag, too. Can you take a blanket and pillow on your bike?"

"I think so. How about Saturday night? Will you meet me down by the road at midnight?"

"Why so late?"

"On account of I'm going to have to sneak out of the house, and Biggie's got ears like a bobcat. I've gotta make sure she's snoring away before I make my move."

"Oh, yeah," Monica said. "Hey, this sounds like fun. We can fish and fry em up at your cabin—and I can slip off and camp out with you. Oh, boy!"

I was beginning to get excited, too. Monica has a way of making you feel anything is possible. "Uh-oh," I said. "I hear Biggie and Rosebud."

We put our cocoa cups in the sink, and when we got to the front hall, Biggie was taking off her gloves.

"Lordy mercy," she said. "That new mayor is as long-winded as Gribbons used to be. I thought he'd never shut up and let the choir sing again. You kids still up?"

"Yes'm," I said, hanging my head.

"J.R.," Biggie said.

"Yes'm?"

"J.R., look at me. What are you up to?"

"Nothin'."

"Well, you look just like the cat that ate the canary. And what's Monica grinning about?"

"Oh, Miss Biggie," Monica said, "I'm just grinning because I had such a good time tonight at the square. It was just so kind of you to invite me. I just wish I could stay here at your house *all the time!*"

Biggie gave Monica a sharp look but didn't ask any more questions. "Okay," she said. "You two hop up to bed. The guest room is made up for Monica. J.R., you see she has clean towels and washcloth."

"Yes'm."

"And, J.R., get a good night's sleep. I've got a list of errands as long as my arm to do tomorrow, and I want you to go with me. Rosebud is taking Monica home early!"

"Yes'm."

18

When I came downstairs the next morning, Biggie was talking on the phone.

"My soul," she said, "I'd forgotten all about it. Um-hmm . . . yes, well, you're sure you can't get anybody else? How about Lonie? Oh, well, that's too bad. No, I said I'd do it. . . . I'll be there by eleven at the latest. Um-hmm, bye."

"What, Biggie?" I said.

Biggie went to the stove and poured herself a cup of coffee. "I forgot today was the day all the churches are getting together to make Christmas baskets for the needy. Lonie can't go because she's in the choir, and they're practicing for the cantata today." She looked at her watch. "We have to be at the community center in one hour."

"We? Not me, Biggie. Uh . . . I gotta help Rosebud rake the yard. Remember? You said so yesterday morning."

Biggie gave me a hard look. "You'd rather clean gutters than help make baskets for poor children? Shame on you, J.R."

"But, Biggie . . . uh, I'll be the only kid . . ."

"No, you won't. Brother Porterfield from the holiness church is sending his youth group, the Royal Knights of Jesus."

"But, Biggie, I don't have much in common with . . ."

I was about to tell Biggie I didn't have much in common with the Royal Knights, who always keep their white shirts buttoned all the way to the top and slick their hair back with greasy stuff, but the phone rang again.

"God bless America! Who is it now? Hello!" Biggie said. "Oh, Paul and Silas . . . no, I'm not mad at you. It's just . . . What? Oh, in that case, you'd better come right over."

Ten minutes later, Paul and Silas was knocking on our back door.

"Wipe your feets," Willie Mae said, pouring him a mug of coffee.

Paul and Silas wiped his feet on the yellow mat by the door and bowed low to Willie Mae as she handed him his coffee. He flopped down at the table and shoved a brown envelope toward Biggie. "The white pages are Firman's autopsy, and the pink are ballistics reports."

Biggie squinted at the pages. "I need my glasses." She looked around the kitchen. "Someone's always moving them."

Willie Mae plucked them off the windowsill over the

sink. "Ain't nobody touched em," she said, handing them to Biggie.

Biggie put the glasses on her nose and stared at the papers. She pushed them back over to Paul and Silas. "Just give me the nuts and bolts. I don't have time to plow through all these words."

Paul and Silas took the papers with a grin. "It says here that Firman died no later than four, which means he'd been dead a good little while before the crowd gathered at the café."

"Hmm," Biggie said, "that changes things a good bit. It would appear to eliminate Dub as a suspect. He was still on his run at that time."

Paul and Silas nodded. "It clears Ben Birdsong, too. I questioned his Mexican helpers. They swear he didn't leave the plant until almost five."

Rosebud had been sitting on a stool by the stove, listening. "I reckon it must cancel out Miss Fairy Lee, too, seein' as how Dub and her both say he picked her up at home at four forty-five," he said.

"Unless one's lying to cover for the other," Biggie said. "What's in the ballistics report?"

Paul and Silas picked up the pink papers. "Okay, here goes. The shell that killed Firman came from the gun J.R. found at Clovis's place."

"I knew it," Biggie said.

"What about the one I picked up in my glop?" I asked.

"A rifle shell," Paul and Silas said, "just like the one ya'll found out at the farm."

"From the same gun?" Biggie asked.

"No, Cousin Biggie. Different guns."

"Biggie," I said, "people hunt in those woods all the time."

"Okay," Biggie said. "The one we found at the farm could have come from some hunter's gun. But it's a lead-pipe cinch nobody was hunting in back of the Fresh-as-a-Daisy café that night."

Biggie got up and went to the desk. She took out the papers and snapshots she'd taken from Firman's apartment. She opened her mouth to say something to Paul and Silas, then looked at me.

"J.R.," she said, "I feel a little tickle in my throat. How about riding your bike down to Plumley's and have him mix up a bottle of his special cough medicine. Tell Dedrick I think I'm coming down with the same thing I had last winter. He'll know what you mean. Have yourself a milk shake while you're there."

Naturally, I knew Biggie had in mind to get rid of me. She'd been acting mysterious ever since she got that stuff from Firman's apartment. But I didn't complain on account of I just love the chocolate-strawberry milk shakes they make down at Mr. Plumley's soda fountain.

By the time I got back, Paul and Silas and Biggie were standing on the front porch.

"Don't forget," Biggie told him, "keep a sharp eye out."

"Never fear, Cousin Biggie," he said. "I won't let them out of my sight."

The community center is a big metal building across the street from the Little League park. It was cold as a frosted

161

frog inside, even though they had the big heaters in the ceiling going full blast. Long folding tables covered with canned goods, frozen turkeys, and toys reached from the front of the room to the big double doors in back that led to the stalls and riding ring where the 4-H kids have their livestock shows. People stood around the tables filling baskets and talking over the sound of the loudspeaker, which was playing Christmas songs.

Biggie put her hands over her ears. "My soul, it's loud in here."

DeWayne Boggs, wearing his Royal Knights white buttoned-up shirt and black pants, came running to the door when we walked in. He was wearing a red banner across his white shirt.

"What's that?" I asked, pointing at his banner.

"It shows I learned the most Bible verses," he said. "You want to come help us?"

"I don't think . . ."

"Sure he does," Biggie said. "Oh, I see the ladies from the altar guild. I'll see you later."

Quick as a wink, she was gone. There was nothing left for me to do but follow DeWayne to a table at the back of the building. The table was surrounded by boys and girls, including DeWayne's sister and brother, Angie Jo and Franklin Joe. A few grown-ups from the holiness church were running things. I was surprised to see Fairy Lee among them.

"Hey, J.R.," she said. "You come to help?"

"I guess," I said.

She shoved a pile of thin plastic Frisbees toward me,

and I saw that everything on the table was arranged in piles—Frisbees, foam footballs, little pocket New Testaments, toothbrushes, combs, and a bunch of other junk. The baskets, already filled with food, were lined up in the middle of the table.

"DeWayne's going to show you all what to do," she said, raising her voice so all the Knights and Knightesses could hear.

"Okay," DeWayne raised his voice so the other kids would listen. I could tell he was real proud of himself for being in charge. "Everybody get in a line. YA'LL LISTEN, NOW!"

The kids looked at him, then went back to jabbering and punching each other.

"Okay," DeWayne said again, "line up over here. Fairy Leeee! They won't do right!"

Fairy Lee and her mother were working our end of the table. Except for her gray hair, which was long and piled on top of her head, Fairy Lee's mother looked a good bit like Fairy Lee. They both wore crosses on little gold chains around their necks, and the mother had big diamonds stuck on her earlobes. They were wearing thin pink blouses with high necks and no makeup. Fairy Lee came over to our side of the table, clapping her hands for attention. After a while, she and her mama got all the kids to stop talking and form a line.

"Now," she said, pointing to the table, "everybody's been assigned a pile. J.R. is Frisbees, DeWayne is combs, Franklin Joe is hair bows. . . ."

"I ain't hair bows," Franklin Joe said. "That's for girls."

"Okay," Fairy Lee said. "Sheneisha, you be hair bows. Franklin Joe can be combs."

"Hey! I'm combs," somebody said.

It took a while, but finally the ladies got everybody sorted out and halfway quiet.

"Now," Fairy Lee said real loud, "line up again and all march around the table singing 'Jesus Loves the Little Children,' and when you come to your pile, drop one of your toys into each basket."

I looked around to see whether anyone I knew was watching, but we seemed to be the only kids in the place. Believe me, I was going to have plenty to say to Biggie when we got home.

When it was finally over and all the piles of stuff were in the baskets, Fairy Lee clapped her hands for attention.

"Now," she said, "it's time for refreshments!"

She dug a glass pickle jar full of green Kool-Aid from an ice chest on the floor. Then she set out a row of the littlest paper cups I'd ever seen outside of someone's bathroom.

When everyone had taken a cup, she said, "Now, let us return thanks."

To my way of thinking, that Kool-Aid wasn't worth half the prayers Fairy Lee said over it. When she finally said "amen" and we all started to sip, she let out a holler that dern near shook the rafters plumb out of that community center.

"My cross!" she yelled. "My diamond cross . . . it's gone!"

We all commenced looking for it on the floor and between the baskets on the table. Fairy Lee was hollering, and her mama was patting her on the shoulder. A crowd began to gather to see what the ruckus was about. Biggie opened her mouth to take charge of the situation, but before she could say anything, Fairy Lee began dumping all the poor people's baskets out on the table and searching through the stuff for her cross. Finally her mother came over and pulled her away.

"Don't worry, honey," she said. "We'll get you another one."

Biggie looked at her with her mouth open. I looked at the table. It was a disaster. Before anyone could stop me, I ran out of the building and crouched down behind Biggie's car. Biggie could beat me to a bloody pulp if she wanted to, but there was nothing in the world that was going to make me help the Knights and Knightesses clean up that mess.

That night after supper, I went straight up to my room. I was mad at Biggie, but maybe that wasn't such a bad thing. After all, wasn't I running away from home? I'd have enough to worry about living off the land without always feeling sorry for myself because I was missing Biggie. I tried to think of other things to be mad about while I undressed, but soon I gave up and started feeling sad again. There's just no denying it, Biggie is about the best grandmother anybody could ask for. I blew my nose on a tissue, and then, as I pulled my shirt off, something shiny fell on the floor. Booger, who had been watching from the top of my chest of drawers, pounced on it and batted it under the bed. When I finally got it away from him, I saw it was Fairy Lee's little cross.

I put my clothes back on and ran down to the den,

where Biggie was watching a Christmas special with Willie Mae and Rosebud. I didn't say anything, just held the cross in front of Biggie's face.

"J.R., stop . . . Oh, heavens! Where did you get that?"

"I didn't steal it, Biggie. Honest."

"Of course you didn't. I only asked you where you got it."

I told her about it falling out of my shirt. "It must have fell in there when she was lining us all up," I said.

"Lemme see that," Willie Mae said. She turned on the floor lamp and held the cross close to the light. "Them's real diamonds. About half carat each, I reckon."

"Couldn't be," Biggie said. "Where would Fairy Lee get something like that?"

"Reckon that Firman give it to her," Rosebud said.

"Biggie, her mama had one on just like it," I said.

Biggie took the cross and turned it over in her hand. "You don't say. Now that's interesting. What would you think it'd bring, Rosebud?"

"Well'm," Rosebud said, taking the cross and squinting at it, "I'm pretty much of an expert on fine jewelry on account of the time me and Brother Theodore used to run us a pawnshop . . ."

"Never mind about that," Biggie said. "How much would you say it's worth?"

"Could be, if them diamonds is real, upward of five figures, I'd say."

Biggie took the cross and locked it in the tin box she keeps in her desk drawer.

"Well," she said, "I think it's time we paid a visit to Fairy Lee *and* her mother."

As it turned out, it was a good while before she had a chance to do that.

19

What's wrong with you, pickin' at your food like that?" Willie Mae asked Saturday morning. She looked hard at me. "I ain't never seen you stop with just one pecan waffle."

"I know what's wrong," Rosebud said, ruffling my hair. "The boy's got a bad case of the hardly waits."

"Huh?" I said.

"You know," Rosebud said, "you cain't hardly wait 'til Christmas mornin'."

"You'd better eat to keep your strength up," Biggie said, cutting into her third waffle. "We have some last-minute shopping to do."

"Okay," I said, "but just one more."

What I was thinking about was not shopping. It was about getting out of bed in that cold cabin Sunday morning with nothing to eat but the few scraps I could steal from Willie Mae's kitchen after the family was asleep. It dern sure wasn't going to be hot pecan waffles with maple syrup. I chewed on the one she dumped on my plate, trying to memorize how it tasted.

Pretty soon, Biggie was telling me to hurry up because we had to get downtown.

The wind was blowing, and Biggie's nose was red as an apple when we got to the square. Mrs. Ben Birdsong, wearing a white coat with a sprig of holly pinned to the collar, almost ran into us. She couldn't see us on account of all the packages she was carrying.

"Excuse me," she said, peering around her packages. "Oh, my, if it isn't Biggie and J.R. Cold enough for ya'll this morning?"

"Colder than a well digger's knee," Biggie said. "How about we all duck into the tearoom and have something to warm our innards."

"Well, I'd sure like to take a load off," Mrs. Ben said. "I've been at this since the stores opened."

Biggie is always dragging me into Mattie's Tearoom, which is about the sissiest place in the whole world. It's painted pink inside with flowerdy curtains, and every one of the tables has its own vase of fake pink roses. Miss Mattie's husband, Norman Thripp, was sitting at one of the tables, wearing a ruffledy apron that matched the curtains and reading the newspaper. He looked up when he heard the bell, then went back to reading his paper.

"Norman!" Miss Mattie said, sticking her head through the little window that leads to the kitchen. "Norman, get up from there and wait on these customers. Hidy, Biggie. Hidy, Laverne. Ya'll just set down anyplace. Norman'll be with you in a minute. Norman!"

169

Mr. Thripp finally shoved his paper aside and came over to our table, carrying three pink menus.

"What can I get ya'll?" he asked like he wasn't really interested.

"I'll take hot chocolate and a sticky bun," I said.

Biggie looked at me. "I see you've got your appetite back. Hmm, I think I'll have hot spiced tea with an apple turnover."

Mrs. Ben ordered the same. She started digging around in one of her sacks. "Ben had me pick up the pictures he took at the grand opening," she said. "Ya'll want to see? There's a right nice one of you, Biggie."

Biggie perked up. "I sure would like to."

Mrs. Ben spread the color shots out on the table. "Look at that Ruby Muckleroy," she said. "She thinks she's hot stuff, don't she?"

"Um-hmm." Biggie held the pictures away from her eyes so she could see.

"You need to get you some glasses, Biggie," Miss Mattie said, walking up to the table. "I got some real nice ones over at Plumley's. Picked em right off the rack."

"I've got some," Biggie said. "I just can't ever find them." She pointed to one of the pictures. "Who's that hiding behind that black van?"

I took the picture and looked at it. "They're not hiding, Biggie. That ain't nobody but old man Threadgill coming around it on his mower."

"*Isn't*," Biggie said absentmindedly. "Laverne, would you mind if I had the negatives to these? There might be important clues hidden here."

Mrs. Birdsong picked up the pictures and stuffed them back in the envelope. "I'll have to ask Ben, but I'm sure he won't mind. Why don't I just drop them in the mail to you?"

"Fine," Biggie said, draining her teacup. "Where's a good place to buy gifts for J.R.'s teachers?"

"I know," Miss Mattie said. "Bert Handy over at the hardware store's got in a shipment of little bitty tool sets. You know, screwdrivers and pliers and a little hammer packed in these cute little wood boxes. I thought they'd just be real nice for a teacher—or anybody else, I guess, to keep in their desk drawer."

"Thanks, Mattie," Biggie said, slapping some bills on the table. "No, Laverne, you put your money away. This one's on me."

Naturally, Mrs. Ben had to argue even though I could have told her she was wasting her breath. Finally she said, "Well, okay, but the next one's on me."

When we got back home Biggie got out her box of Christmas wrappings and told me I had to wrap the five little toolboxes because they were for my teachers. When I got through, Rosebud said they didn't look any better than that wrapped-up barbecue he's always bringing home from Odie's Place. I didn't care. The way I figured it, I'd be out at the creek living off the land when school started back up again.

I went into the kitchen to talk to Willie Mae. "What's for supper?" I asked.

"I only just begun washin' up from lunch, and here you be askin' about supper."

"I was just makin' conversation."

Willie Mae turned from the sink and looked at me. "How come you ain't down at the park playin' ball?"

"Well, gol-ee, can't a person stay home with his own family once in a while?"

"What's got into you?"

"Nothin'," I said, getting up from the table.

Willie Mae dried her hands on the dish towel. "Come set back down. You want some milk?"

"No'm."

"Set back down." She pulled out chairs for her and me. "What do you want for supper?"

I thought for a minute. "Fried chicken with lots of leftovers," I said, "and mashed potatoes and gravy and red Jell-O with bananas and, uh—I know, roasting ears!"

Willie Mae gave me a look I couldn't understand, then stared at me until little points of light seemed to shoot straight at me from her eyeballs. It made a rabbit hop over my grave. Then she spoke real slow. "You gonna run away, ain't you?"

"Naw, not me."

"Ain't you?"

I got up and ran to my room as fast as I could and slammed the door. I stood for a minute listening for her footsteps coming up the back stairs, but all I heard was Biggie's soft snoring from her room across the hall.

I spent the afternoon packing my stuff. First I laid everything out on my bed. There was my collection of *Goosebumps* books, my shells that I collected at Padre Island, my framed pictures of my mama and daddy and one of Biggie holding me on her lap when I was a baby, the picture of me and Rosebud holding up the five-pound bass I caught last summer, my pajamas, my pillow, my quilt, and a change of clothes. Last, I threw a clean pair of socks on the pile. The stuff covered my whole bed. When I got out my backpack, it was pretty obvious I wasn't going to be able to take everything, so I just put in the picture of Biggie and my clothes. I got out my money and shoved that in, and thinking it would make Biggie feel better when she came and found me gone, I stuck in my toothbrush. I rolled my pillow in my quilt and strapped it tight with my belt. I guessed that could ride on the back of my bike.

Willie Mae made exactly what I asked for for supper, except the roasting ears, which she said weren't in season. She made lima beans instead. I eyeballed the platter of fried chicken in the middle of the table. The way I figured it, if Rosebud didn't go and make a hog of himself, I should have over half a chicken to take with me.

The evening went by slower than a three-legged turtle. Biggie dozed in her chair. Rosebud was working a crossword puzzle, and Willie Mae had gone to their little house in the backyard as soon as supper was over. Finally Biggie woke with a little jump and got up out of her chair.

"My soul," she said, "ten o'clock already." She headed for the stairs. " 'Night, Rosebud. J.R., I'll be in to say good night as soon as I've had my bath."

As soon as I heard Biggie turn on her bathwater, I ran up to my room and started shoving the pile of stuff under my bed. Next, I put on some pajamas over my clothes and crawled under the covers. I waited until Biggie came in. She leaned over and gave me a kiss.

"Why do you have your pajamas buttoned up to your neck like that?" she asked.

"I'm just cold."

"Want me to turn up the thermostat?"

"No'm."

"Well, there's another blanket in the hall closet. Sleep tight."

"Yes'm."

It wasn't long before I could hear Biggie snoring away. I eased out of bed, being careful on account of my bed's got squeaky springs. Next I put on my wool sweater, then my fleece-lined jacket, took my genuine wool baseball cap off the top of my bureau and gathered up my backpack and bedroll. I looked around to see if I'd forgotten anything and saw my glop in its plastic bag on my desk. I stuck that in my pocket and eased myself out into the hall and tiptoed down the back stairs. I got a plastic grocery sack out of the pantry and opened the refrigerator door. Willie Mae had put the leftover chicken in a plastic bag, which I thought was strange since she usually uses a Tupperware bowl. I put the bag in my grocery sack. Then I poked around looking for more stuff. I found a few cold biscuits, a couple of apples, and just as I was closing my sack, I spied a plate of banana nut muffins on the counter. I threw three of those in and tiptoed out the back door.

I stayed close to the house on account of it was a bright, moonlit night. I tied my bedroll to the back fender of my bike and hung my food sack over the handlebars. Just as I was riding away, I could have sworn I saw the curtain move in Willie Mae and Rosebud's little house.

There wasn't a single car in sight as I pedaled out of

town. That's on account of they roll up the sidewalks in Job's Crossing by ten o'clock. As I passed the park and the intermediate school, I tried not to think about how I wouldn't be seeing them again for a long time. I felt a little better after I passed the city limit sign—free, somehow. Now I started thinking about starting a new life as a hermit. I sure hoped Monica hadn't forgotten how she promised to meet me at the gate to the farm so we could go to the cabin together.

The wind was cold, but not too cold on my face as I rode along, and I started singing the school fight song to keep myself company. Just as I got to the part that says, "Go, Great Gobblers! Fight! Fight! Fight," I saw two bright headlights speeding toward me. I steered my bike onto the shoulder to get out of the way. The car swerved the same way until it was heading straight for me and kept coming—fast.

What happened next was not a pretty sight.

20

I leaped off my bike and rolled into the ditch as the car skidded to a stop not an inch from where I'd been. I hunkered down in the darkness, praying whoever it was wouldn't steal my brand-new bike. The car doors slammed, and two long shadows appeared on the frosty grass on the opposite slope.

Then a voice spoke, one I knew too well. "Gawdamighty! Ain't that the kid's bike?"

It was those Culpeppers. I didn't know what else to do, so I crawled up the bank and stood in front of them, rubbing my arm where it had hit a rock when I dry-dived into that ditch.

Jane threw her arms around me and hugged me to her. She smelled like cigarettes and beer. "Looky here," she said, "how come you to be out here on the road and it damn near midnight?"

I thought fast. "I gotta go," I said. "Biggie's had a heart attack, and I'm goin' for the doctor."

"You ain't much of a liar," she said. "Now, what do you reckon would've happened to you if we hadn't decided to tilt a few down at the Dewdrop Inn? You could've got yourself killed."

"Please," I said, "I gotta go. Really!"

She turned to Skinny. "Open up the trunk and put that bicycle inside. We might just as well take this kid and head on back north this very night."

Skinny nodded and reached for my bike.

"B-but wait," I said, trying to keep from bawling, "you can't go until the crime's solved. Biggie said . . ."

The mention of Biggie's name just got her mad all over. She shook her finger at me. "Biggie, Biggie, Biggie," she said real nasty. "Well, let me tell you somethin', young'un. You might just as well forget you ever heard of Biggie Weatherford on account of when we get to Montana, you ain't never going to see her again. Got that? And if that old woman tries to stop me, I'll have her drug into court for child neglect. Now get in that backseat this very minute—or else!"

I got.

Skinny got in the driver's side, whistling between his teeth like he always does. Before he cranked up the engine, he turned and winked at me.

I curled up in the corner of the leather seat and looked out at the frosty night. The moon shone almost as bright as day. I wondered if Monica was standing out in the cold waiting for me. Then I thought of something. Maybe she'd get worried and call Biggie. Maybe they were searching for me already. But I knew that wasn't going to happen. There's one thing about Monica. She can keep a secret. I'd told her not to tell, and I knew they could torture her until she was stone cold dead, and she'd never rat on me.

Suddenly Jane let out a holler. "Stop this car!" she said. "Hand me that rifle out of the back, kid. Hurry!"

"Huh?" I said.

"The rifle. It's on the rack in the rear window. Give it here. I'm gonna shoot me a chicken hawk."

Skinny pulled the car onto the shoulder and stopped while I lifted the rifle from the rack and passed it over to Jane, wondering why she wanted to do that.

I looked out the window, and sure enough, there was a great big hawk sitting on top of a dead tree snag. She drew a bead on the bird and squeezed the trigger. The hawk just toppled off the tree and dropped to the ground. I watched as a few feathers floated down after him.

Jane ejected the shell and pushed another bullet in the chamber. I was interested in spite of myself.

"I never saw a rifle like that before," I said.

"It's an old army gun," she said. "Here, put it back."

After a little while, I could see the lights of the convenience store and the motel as Skinny turned the car onto the bypass. He pulled into the motel parking lot and stopped in front of their room. There were no more cars on that lot. The Big Eight doesn't get many customers except when they have the bass fishing tournament in August.

"Okay, kid," Jane said as she slid the key into the door of the motel room. "Sit over there on the bed and stay out of the way while we pack."

I wrinkled my nose as I pushed some junk over to sit on

the bed. The room smelled like the rest room at the filling station mixed in with cheap perfume.

"And, by the way," she said over her shoulder, "your name's not J.R. anymore. From now on, you'll be Ernest Ray Culpepper—Little Skinny for a nickname. Ain't that cute, Skinny? You can be Big Skinny, and the kid here can be Little Skinny."

Skinny nodded and went on sticking stuff into his shaving kit.

Jane was taking things out of the dresser drawers and stuffing them in her suitcase. "Where the hell's my brassiere?" she said, looking around the room. "Oh, I see it. The kid's sittin' on it." She pulled the big old thing out from under where I was sitting. "Get on out and wait in the car," she said to me. "I can't find nothin' with you in the way."

I got behind the steering wheel and pretended I was driving far away from there. I couldn't see a way to escape. The motel room wasn't five feet away from where I was sitting, and the door was open. They would catch me in two seconds flat if I made a run for it. I pulled my glop out of my pocket and started mooshing it around in my hands. Pretty soon, Skinny came out and loaded two bags into the trunk, then went back inside. If there was only a way I could delay things, I thought. Then maybe, just maybe, Biggie would discover I was gone and come looking for me.

Suddenly I had an idea. I looked in the door of the room. Jane was stuffing towels and sheets into a pillowcase. Next, she rinsed out the ashtrays and threw them in. Skinny had gone in the bathroom and closed the door. I pinched off a little piece of my glop and stuffed it in the ignition switch. When I pressed it with my finger, it disappeared, so I put a little more in. I kept stuffing glop into that little hole until it was full. Then I smoothed it off with my finger so you couldn't tell was there. Just as I finished, I heard the motel room door slam.

"Get in the back, kid," Jane said, glaring at me. "You ain't riding up here."

I crawled into the backseat and waited to see what would happen when Skinny tried to start the car. He stuck the key in the switch a little way, then started wiggling it and pushing harder.

"Well, come on," Jane said. "We gotta make the Oklahoma line before we can stop and get some rest."

Skinny looked at her and shrugged. For the first time, he wasn't whistling between his teeth.

"Lemme see that thing," Jane said.

She tried to ram the key in, then said some words I'd seen written on bathroom walls. She turned toward me.

"What did you do?" she said real soft and slow.

"Nothin', honest." Naturally, I had my fingers crossed.

I never in my life saw a fat woman move so fast. In a flash, she was out of that car and had the back door open. She grabbed me by the arm and yanked me out, then held me up until I was eyeball to eyeball with her. I could smell her beer breath and body odor, but that was the least of my worries. I knew I was about to die. I tried to think of some prayers I'd heard at church, but all I could think of was the blessing we say at the table when company comes. And somehow "Bless this food to the nourishment of our bodies" didn't seem appropriate, so I just closed my eyes and waited for her fist to come crashing down on my face.

I thought I heard a car drive up and doors slam, but I

kept my eyes shut tight. Then I heard Biggie's voice, and I knew I'd either died and gone to heaven or been saved. Either way, it seemed safe to open my eyes. When I did, I saw Biggie and Rosebud standing there glaring at Jane. Slowly she set me down. I ran to Biggie.

"Biggie, they were taking me to Montana!" I said.

"Janie Pearl," Biggie said, "I always knew you were so dumb you didn't know spit from noodles, but this is about the stupidest thing you've ever tried to pull. Did you really think I'd allow you to just drive off with J.R.?"

Jane tried to sound brave, but her voice shook. "I got a piece of paper . . ." she began.

"And I've got one, too," Biggie said. "I think it's best we all go back inside that motel room and have a little chat."

She headed for the door, and the others followed. I suddenly felt weak in the knees and started to fall. Rosebud picked me up and carried me in, then sat on a chair with me on his knee. When the others had taken a seat, Biggie started in talking.

"Now," she said, "I think it's time Skinny explained why he came to town with the intention of shooting Firman Birdsong."

I waited for Jane to speak for him, but she just sat with her mouth open.

Finally, for the first time, Skinny spoke. "Reckon it's true," he said in a high squeaky voice. "I had a mind to blow out his lamp."

"Mind tellin' us why?" Rosebud asked.

"I expect Biggie already knows," Skinny said.

"Shut up, Skinny. Just shut up!" Jane said.

"You're right," Biggie said, ignoring Jane. "I suspected

when I found a snapshot of the three of you in Firman's things. I was sure after I wrote to the bureau of vital statistics in Montana. Firman was the scoundrel who fathered your grandchild, wasn't he?"

"That's right," Jane said. "But Skinny didn't kill him. Tell her, Skinny."

Skinny hung his head. "It weren't because I didn't try. I watched that restaurant until I seen him drive up with his two Mes'cans and go in the kitchen door. It was early— around four, I reckon. I waited until it got near dark, then took my rifle over and hid myself behind the Dumpster figurin' I might draw a bead on him. The trouble was, the heat in the kitchen had done fogged up the windows so I couldn't hardly see a thing. I thought I seen old Firman walk up to the window, so I let go a shot at him. By that time, folks had begun to show up around there. It was too risky to try again, so I figured I'd have to wait my chance to plug him later."

"But he didn't," Jane put in. "Tell her, Skinny."

"Wellsir," he said, "I was mighty curious to see whether I'd hit him, so I took my chances and snuck up to the back door and put my head in. Them Mes'cans had gone out back to that big walk-in freezer they got for a load of frozen dinners, so I snuck inside, and there he was, layin' underneath the table, dead as a hammer. I'm mighty dry."

Jane dug down into her purse and pulled out a half-pint bottle of whiskey. She handed it to him, and he poured about half of it down his throat.

He coughed a little, then continued. "Well, unless somebody had come along and moved him, I knew my bullet hadn't kilt him on account of he was over behind the big stove pushed up under a table. I kicked him with my foot. It was then I spied a big pot of gravy on the stove. I taken it and poured it all over him, then decorated him up with tomaters and parsley. That's the livin' truth, Biggie. I swear it."

"I know," Biggie said. "Firman was killed with a revolver, not a rifle." She stood up. "Well, two things can happen here. I can have you thrown in jail for attempted murder, or you two can get out of town and never come back. If you even so much as think of trying to take J.R. again . . ." Biggie's voice broke.

They both shook their heads.

"Then that's it," Biggie said. "Let's go home."

"Can I ask one thing?" I said.

Biggie nodded.

I turned to my other grandmother. "Did ya'll come here to get me, or to kill Mr. Birdsong?"

"Hell, Skinny wanted to get old Firman. We didn't even know you was here 'til we stopped off in Dallas to say hidy to your ma. That's when I got the idea you might be a good replacement for the kid Skinny lost. Shoot, I didn't care one way or the other."

"Let's go," I said.

"Where's your bike?" Rosebud asked.

"I don't want that old thing," I said, picking up my bedroll and backpack. "My old one's good enough."

21

When we pulled into our driveway, Willie Mae was standing at the back door watching for us. She was wrapped in her red silk scarf with the black dragon that Sister Sylvester had given her when she graduated voodoo school.

"Come in the kitchen," she said, giving me a face-scrunching hug. "I got you some hot cocoa on the stove."

"Can we drink it in the den with the Christmas tree lights on?" I asked.

Biggie looked at the clock on the wall. It said 12:40. "Sure, I guess so. You and Rosebud go and plug in the tree. I'll help Willie Mae make up a tray."

I curled up on the corner of the couch while Rosebud stretched out in the big leather easy chair that used to belong to my grandpa. I looked at the tree. For a minute, it felt like the little white lights were smiling and winking just for me. I saw the crooked paper snowman I'd made in first grade and the picture of me framed in a mason jar ring that I'd made in Bible school when I was eight. I remembered how Biggie always keeps those two ornaments in a silver box on her dresser instead of letting them be tossed in the carton with the other trimmings when the tree comes down. I thought about how, if I'd gone to Montana with those Culpeppers, Biggie'd probably be bawling her eyes out when she put them away this year. I felt a little lump start to form in my throat.

Rosebud got up to punch the fire with the poker. "Hand me another log," he said, pointing to the wood basket, "and tell me how come you be lookin' like the cheese just fell off your cracker."

Before I could open my mouth to answer, Willie Mae came into the room carrying a tray with mugs of hot chocolate and a plate piled high with hot cinnamon toast. Biggie was right behind her.

"Drink up. It's near one o'clock." She stood with her back to the fire and looked first at me and then at Rosebud and Willie Mae. "There's no place like home with your family," she said.

I took a big bite of cinnamon toast, and just as I was about to raise my mug to drink, the windows shook, and we all jumped as a noise that sounded just like an explosion went off in our driveway. Right after that, I heard a door slam, and someone ran up on the porch and started banging on the front door. When Rosebud flung open the door, Monica came rushing into the room. She was wearing her daddy's hunting clothes and her hat with the flaps on the sides. It was lopsided on her head.

She ran straight to Biggie. "Miss Biggie," she said, panting, "J.R.'s . . ."

Then she saw me, and before I could duck, she was on top of me, hitting me all over with both fists.

"Hey! Quit!" I yelled. "Get her off me!"

"Whoa!" Rosebud said and picked Monica up, holding her in the air. Her fists were still swinging and her feet kicking. "What's got into you, child?" he asked.

"Put me down!" Monica yelled. "Let me at him."

"Not until you tell me what's got you all riled up."

I rubbed my chin where she'd dern near busted it and looked at Monica. "I got kidnapped," I said. "That's why I didn't come."

All of a sudden, the steam seemed to drain out of her. She stopped swinging, and Rosebud set her down on the sofa next to me.

Willie Mae poured Monica a mug of cocoa.

Then Biggie spoke up. "Now, then. What's going on here?"

After we'd explained all about our plans for me to live in the cabin, Biggie sighed. "I never knew you were so upset. Didn't I tell you I'd never let you go?"

"Yes'm, but . . ."

"Never mind. Monica, what was that god-awful noise we heard?"

"That wasn't nothing but Pa's old truck backfiring." Monica drained her mug and stood up. "Now I think about it, I best be getting on back. Pa'll have my hide if he finds it missing."

"Nope," Biggie said. "You had no business driving it on

the road at your age. I understand that you were worried about J.R., but that's no excuse."

"Miss Biggie!" Monica wailed. "Pa'll have a cow if I don't get that truck back."

"I'll telephone your parents and explain everything," Biggie said. "In the morning, Rosebud will drive the truck home, and I'll follow in the car. Tonight, you'll sleep in our guest room. I'll even loan you one of my nightgowns to wear. Now hop upstairs, you two. I'll be up in a minute."

Later, when Biggie came up to say good night, Monica was already snoring away in the guest room.

Biggie hugged me so long I had to start squirming to get her to let me go.

"I'm sorry," she said. "I know you don't like too much hugging." She shivered. "It's just that I was worried about you, J.R."

"Biggie, how did you know to come looking for me?"

"Willie Mae saw you go."

"But how did you know to come to the motel?"

"That's a funny thing, J.R. Rosebud figured you'd go straight to the farm and Monica. I thought you might be at someone's house here in town, so first we cruised the streets where your friends live, looking for your bike. When we didn't see it, we decided to start for the farm. Rosebud took the bypass out of town because it's the shortest route. It was pure luck that we passed the motel just in time to see that woman shaking you." Her hands balled up in fists. "If I ever see either of them again . . . Oh, well, I'm tuckered out, and you are, too." She leaned over and kissed me before I could duck. " 'Night, honey."

I was asleep before she closed the door.

The next morning when I came down, Willie Mae had already cleared away the breakfast things.

"Where's Biggie?" I asked, taking a cold biscuit off the back of the stove.

"Gone to take Monica home. You want me to make you some eggs?" Willie Mae said.

"Huh?"

"You heard me. You want some eggs?"

"No'm," I said, taking a banana to go with my biscuit. I figured Willie Mae must be really glad to have me home on account of she's got a rule that says if you don't come to breakfast on time, you have to wait until lunch to eat. I've never in my life seen her break that rule. Now here she was offering to cook a special breakfast just for me. I covered up a grin with my hand.

"How come you grinnin' like a possum?" she asked.

"Uh, I just thought of something. I gotta go to the bathroom," I said, running from the room.

"Don't you take no food in that bathroom. . . ."

I didn't hear the rest because I'd run out the front door and flopped down on the porch swing.

The wind had changed. Now it was blowing from the south, and the sun was hidden behind wispy clouds. The air felt muggy but warm, a sure sign we'd get rain, then another norther. I was thinking maybe we'd get a white Christmas when Butch came walking fast up the sidewalk toward our house.

"Where's Biggie?" he asked, blowing and puffing from hurrying so. "Ooh, there she comes. Biggeee!"

Just then, our car pulled into the driveway.

Biggie got out and came up the porch steps. She was wearing jeans and a red sweatshirt with a sprig of holly pinned to the front.

"Biggie, thank the Lord you're here. Wait 'til you hear what I just this minute heard down at Handy's House of Hardware. I rushed right straight over so you'd be the first to know—after me, of course . . . and Bert Handy, who heard it from his wife, who got it right from Ruby Muckleroy herself."

Biggie sank down on a rocker and motioned for Butch to do the same. "Sit down, honey, and tell Biggie all about it."

"Well"—Butch kind of blew the word out, like a sigh—"Ruby is fit to be tied! She told Miz Handy she might just as well pack up and move to Ore City or somewhere like that because it's a cinch she'll never be able to hold her head up in this town again!"

"My goodness, what's got Ruby so stirred up?"

"Well, you know her brother Wilson? The one she don't talk about very much?"

"Sure. He lives up around Talco, doesn't he?"

"Yeah," Butch said. "Well, that young man went and got himself F.W.I.'d."

"What?" Biggie asked.

"F.W.I.'d," Butch repeated. "Flying While Intoxicated!"

"My soul, how'd he do that?"

Butch wiggled in his seat. "See, here's what happened. Old Wilson had gone and got himself one of those airplanes that you can buy in barrels."

"What?"

"Yeah, Biggie. They sell the parts and you can build

189

your own plane. It's cheaper that way. Anyway, Wilson got his plane built . . . rented a barn from some farmer to use for a hangar, then he hired this towheaded kid from up around Sugar Hill, and the two of them went into the crop-dusting business. Well, they were crop dusting an old boy's soybeans one day last summer, and it was awful dry up there what with all that dust blowing and all, so this kid just happened to have a jar of homemade whiskey that his daddy had made, and him and Wilson started in sipping on it . . . just to wet their whistles, is what they told the trooper that arrested them."

"Last summer?" Biggie said. "My word, Butch, that's old news."

"No, it's not," Butch said. "See, nobody around here would've ever found out if it hadn't been a slow news week last week. Julia Lockhart was looking for something to put in her column, so she got the idea to check the arrest records in Titus County and just happened to run across it."

"I see. And she was going to print it?"

"Well, no, but it was too good to keep to herself, so she told a few of her closest friends and it got back to Ruby. Now, will you please let me finish? See, what happened was, they both ended up drunk as Cooter Brown and decided to buzz the interstate. They were flying low over the cars and hollering cuss words out the window of the plane . . . and there's more."

"Golly," I said. "What else?"

Butch sighed. "That's what I don't know. Just as Bert was about to tell about Wilson mooning a car full of ladies, Dedrick Plumley came running in and said a woman had had a stroke out at Fresh-as-a-Daisy café and I'd better get the ambulance over there right fast. Naturally, I know my duty. . . ."

"Who was it?" Biggie wanted to know.

"Oh, it wasn't anything much. One of those holiness women, Fairy Lee's mama, had this little old fainting spell was all. By the time I got there she was sitting up drinking coffee and said she'd be all right if I'd just take her on home. So that's what I did."

"What caused her to faint?" Biggie asked.

"How should I know, Biggie? I'm no doctor. Anyway, I was in a hurry to get on back to the hardware store to hear the rest of the story, but by the time I got there, Bert had gotten busy with customers and didn't have time to talk."

"Hmmm. Maybe I'll just drop by to see how she's doing this afternoon." Biggie looked at her watch. "My gracious, it's lunchtime. Would you like to join us, Butch?"

"What are you having?"

"Liver and onions," I said, "with rice and gravy and squash casserole."

"I can't eat liver," Butch said. "It just lays there on my stomach for hours." He stood up. "Well, I'd better go. I'll let you know if I hear any more, Biggie."

"You do that," Biggie said, but I could tell by the way she said it she had something else on her mind.

22

"Willie Mae, have you got any more of those little loaves of cranberry bread you made?" Biggie asked as she helped Willie Mae clear away the lunch dishes.

"I reckon," Willie Mae said over the sound of water running into the sink, "we got six or eight loaves left after you give em out to all them Daughters."

"Good. How about fig preserves?"

"Plenty of that, too."

"Are you hungry, Biggie?" I asked.

"No. I just thought it might to be nice to take a little gift basket over to Mrs. Tubbs, Fairy Lee's mother. It seems the Christian thing to do, since the poor woman fainted dead away at the café this morning."

Willie Mae left the sink and started rummaging around in the pantry. She started in pulling out jars of homemade stuff.

"Here's some sweet pickles," she said, "and how about we put in some of them cheese straws I made yesterday—and a little of this here fudge?"

"How come you want to take something over there, Biggie?" I asked. "You don't hardly know that woman."

"Detectin', son, just more detectin'," Rosebud said, sticking his head in the door from the back porch where he'd been sharpening his pocket knife. "Ain't that right, Miss Biggie."

Biggie grinned. "You know me too well, Rosebud. How about driving us over there after I've had a little nap? J.R., go upstairs and get your Easter basket from last year. We can put the stuff in there."

"Biggie, I'm twelve years old. I ain't had an Easter basket in I don't know how long."

"My goodness, that's right," she said, too busy to tell me not to say *ain't*. "Well, don't you have an old one?"

"No'm."

Willie Mae reached in the pantry and pulled out a little pasteboard box. It had "Heinz Tomato Ketchup" printed on the side. "How 'bout we put it in this?" she asked.

"How come they call it *tomato* ketchup?" I asked. "Is there any other kind?"

"That might work," Biggie said. "If we decorate it a little." She pulled a roll of foil out of the drawer and tore a big sheet off it.

"Lemme do that," Willie Mae said. She set the box in the middle of the foil and started folding it up the sides.

"Why not just ketchup?" I asked.

"Wait," Biggie said, "I'll go get a bow."

Rosebud came back in the kitchen testing his pocket

knife on his thumb. "Sharp enough to shave a gnat," he said. "They's plenty of kinds of ketchup. You never heard of okra ketchup?" He winked at Willie Mae. "That's the best kind on account of it just slides right out of the bottle— don't get stuck like the other."

"Go on!" I said.

"Yessiree, okra ketchup. I recollect a time when okra ketchup saved a feller's life." Rosebud poured himself a cup of coffee and sat down at the table. "He was drivin' a okra ketchup truck right outside of Vidor, Texas—"

"There," Biggie said, holding up the silver box with a red bow stuck to the side, "looks nice and Christmasy. Come to think of it, I don't feel tired anymore. Let's just go right on over to Mrs. Tubbs's house this very minute."

"I'll tell you about okra ketchup another time," Rosebud said, reaching for the car keys from the hook by the door. "You comin', boy?"

"I guess."

As we were driving to Mrs. Tubbs's house, I thought of something.

"Biggie," I asked, "how come you knew Mr. Firman was the daddy of old Skinny's grandson? I mean, I know you wrote out to Montana for the birth records, but how did you know to do that in the first place?"

"Oh, didn't I tell you? It was Firman's photos. Remember, there was one picture of Firman as a kid with Skinny and Jane at the rodeo?"

"Yes'm."

"Well, that was the first time I knew those three had known each other in the past. Then when I saw those pic-

194

tures Firman had taken on his trip—the ones of pretty girls—well, the girl on the horse looked a lot like Skinny, black hair and all. Of course, I might not have noticed that if I hadn't already seen the rodeo shot first. I'll admit, I was pretty desperate to find *something* on old Skinny and Jane."

"I'm sure glad you did, Biggie."

"Umm," Biggie said, "turn right here, Rosebud. It's the house on the end of this street, I think."

We'd turned onto a street with no sidewalks. Little frame houses were on either side with a few vacant lots in between. A man was in one of the yards spray-painting a bass boat. Rosebud slowed in front of the only house on the street without a single Christmas light out front. A big black Suburban was parked in the dirt driveway.

"Wait! Drive on past," Biggie said when she spotted the Suburban. "Go to the end of the block and drive around to the street behind this one."

"What, Biggie?" I asked.

"Stop under this tree," Biggie said. "I have to think."

Rosebud stopped the car under a big sycamore tree but kept the motor idling. "What's goin' on?" he asked.

"It's that Suburban," she said. "Where have I seen that car?"

"That's easy, Biggie," I said. "It was in that picture Mrs. Ben had. You know, Mr. Threadgill was riding his lawn mower around the side of it."

"You're right!" Biggie said. "Now who could be visiting Mrs. Tubbs driving that car? Have you ever seen it around town, J.R.?"

"Seems like, but I can't remember when."

"You, Rosebud?"

195

"Nope, and I'd've remembered. That's a mighty fine looking set of wheels—expensive, too."

Biggie cupped her chin in her hand and stared out the window. "There's something playing around in the back of my mind, and I can't quite . . . Wait a minute! Do you two remember the day old Clovis died? We were driving away from his house and E. C. Isom came by on his tractor. . . ."

"Right," Rosebud said. "You asked if he'd seen anybody around the place, and he said . . ."

"A big black car!" I said. "Biggie, he said he saw someone leaving there in a big black car. This is a big black car. It just isn't a *car* car."

"Exactly," Biggie said. "Rosebud, cut off the engine. If we walk through that vacant lot over there, we'll come to Mrs. Tubbs's backyard. I'd like to take a peek through the window before we show ourselves."

"Shall I bring the goody box?" I asked.

"No, leave it," Biggie said. "We'll come back and get it after we find out who's visiting Mrs. Tubbs."

We had to jump a ditch to get to the vacant lot. It was full of oily-looking water. Rosebud crossed first, then stuck out his hand to help Biggie and then me. The lot was grown up with dead weeds and sticker burrs. The yard next door was surrounded by a chain-link fence, and inside was the meanest-looking dog I'd ever seen. It started barking and lunging at the fence when it saw us.

"Eeeyew," I said.

"Don't worry," Rosebud said. "He can't get outta his yard."

But I noticed that Rosebud kept his eye peeled in the dog's direction.

Mrs. Tubbs's yard had a rickety old garage and an unpainted picket fence across the back. Concrete stepping-stones led to the door of the screened-in back porch. A yellow cat stuck his head out through a hole in the screen and meowed at us.

"Don't go to the door yet," Biggie said. "Let's find a window we can look through. Be quiet, now!"

We walked to the side of the house, and Rosebud looked in a window. "Nobody in here," he said. "Looks like a bedroom."

The only window at the back of the house was small and high.

"That must be the window over the kitchen sink," Biggie said, pointing. "Rosebud, you check the other side. Maybe there's a sitting room or something. We'll wait here."

Rosebud tiptoed around the house while we stood watching. He peered into a larger window, then motioned for us to come. He held his finger to his lips.

The window was low enough for me and Biggie to see through if we stood on tiptoe. It was covered with a white lace curtain. When I saw what was going on inside, I had to clap my hands over my mouth to keep from yelping. Mrs. Tubbs was sitting at a round wooden table facing the window. Across from her, back to the window, sat someone wearing a black coat and a stocking cap. And that person was pointing a little silver gun straight at Mrs. Tubbs. Mrs. Tubbs's eyes got big when she saw us, but Biggie motioned for her to keep quiet.

"Come on," Biggie whispered, stepping away from the window. "The back door."

Rosebud went in first, opening the back screen without a sound. The cat jumped down off a bench and wrapped himself around my ankles. Rosebud went to the door that must have led to the kitchen and turned the knob real easy. He disappeared into the kitchen, and in no time he had crossed the room, and before you could say boo to a goose, he'd grabbed Mrs. Ben Birdsong in a big bear hug and was holding on for dear life.

23

Biggie bent to pick up the little silver pistol that had gone sliding across the polished wood floor.

"Put her down, Rosebud," she said. "She can't hurt anybody now."

Rosebud set Mrs. Ben back in the chair but stayed close by on account of she was shaking like a leaf.

"Calm down, Laverne," Biggie said. She turned to Mrs. Tubbs. "You okay, Billie Faye?"

"Praise Jesus," Mrs. Tubbs said. "He sent you in the very nick of time. I could hear the heavenly choir."

"Huh?" I said.

"She thought she was a goner, son," Rosebud whispered to me.

Biggie sat down at the table between the two women. She looked around the room, and for the first time I noticed something. The inside of the house wasn't a bit like the outside. The table was so shiny I could see myself in it, and in the middle set a big silk flower arrangement. A crystal chandelier hung down over it. I saw a china cabinet against the wall packed full of fancy glasses and dishes. The adjoining room must have been the living room, and it was just as fancy as this one, with couches covered in velvet and glass lamps that still had the cellophane wrapped around the shades. The carpet was thick and bright blue.

"You have some nice things, Billie Faye," Biggie said softly.

"The Lord provides," Mrs. Tubbs said.

"The Lord, nothing," Mrs. Ben said. "It's me that's done the providing for going on twenty years—scrimping and saving out of my spending money and lying to Ben . . . and her sending it straight in to that home shopping channel on TV to buy diamond jewelry and a lot of junk to put in this house."

"Blackmail?" Biggie asked.

"That's right," Mrs. Ben said, glaring at Mrs. Tubbs. "And I reckon I'd be paying still if that miff-minded brother-in-law of mine hadn't gone and upset the applecart."

"What are you saying, Laverne?" Biggie asked.

Mrs. Ben let out a sigh and looked at Biggie. "I reckon there's no reason not to tell you. I'd be a fool not to know when the jig's up." She put her elbows on the table and rested her chin in her hands, looking Biggie straight in the eyes. "It all started twenty years ago. I had one of them nervous breakdowns. For days on end, I wouldn't do a thing but just lay in bed with the shades drawn—sunup to sundown. Even lost my taste for shopping—that's how bad it was."

"Seems like I remember hearing about that," Biggie said.

"Probably so," she said, "the way folks talk in this town. Well, Ben seemed like he was real concerned about me at first—taken good care of me, bringing home candy and Cokes and stuff. But I just seemed to get bluer and bluer. Finally, I guess he just got tired—you know—tired of me not performing my, uh, wifely duties. You'd never know it to look at him now, but Ben used to be a regular old rooster."

Mrs. Tubbs blushed. "He was a young man at the time," she said, "and I hadn't received salvation yet."

"You had an affair?" Biggie asked.

"That's right, an affair," Mrs. Ben said. "Back then, you'd never know she was going to turn out to be the sanctimonious, Bible-thumping hypocrite she is now. She kept herself all painted up like a circus clown . . . bleached blond hair . . . cheap dimestore pearls."

"My oh my," Rosebud said.

"And Fairy Lee was the result of that affair," Biggie said, nodding her head.

"That's right," Mrs. Tubbs said. "Nobody would've never known about it on account of I was married at the time myself. Only, when my husband found out I was pregnant, he took off and never came back." She took a tissue out of her pocket and blew her nose. "What could I do? I wrote Ben a letter asking for help—"

"That's right," Mrs. Ben interrupted. "I reckon the silly

fool thought he'd just divorce me and marry her. Thank the Lord I got the letter before Ben did. I come right on over so me and her could have us a little talk. I explained about how Ben wasn't never going to divorce me on account of I'd get half his money, and everybody knows Ben's tighter than paint."

"Um-hmm," Biggie nodded.

"Well, not being what you call a hard woman, I said I'd let her do some sewing for me. She's real good at it, you know. And I told all my friends about her. Pretty soon, she had a right nice little business going."

"Humph!" Mrs. Tubbs said. "Easy for you to say, livin' up there in your big brick house, drivin' your fancy cars."

Mrs. Ben ignored that. "So, one day when I'd come over for a fitting, she lets it drop that she needs more money, and I'm the one that's going to give it to her, or she'll go to Ben. Well, naturally, I didn't want Ben to find out I'd read his mail. So, out of the kindness of my heart, I started giving her what I could from time to time. If you want to know what I think, I think there ain't many women that'd do what I did for their husband's fancy woman and her bastard child."

"Shoot," Mrs. Tubbs said. "You were scared he'd leave you for me, and all your highbrow friends would know you couldn't keep a man."

"So," Biggie said to Mrs. Ben, "she kept coming back for more and more money. Right?"

"Right," Mrs. Ben said. "And she'd still be bleeding me if Firman hadn't brought things to a head by getting all googly-eyed over the girl. It was when he started going on about marrying her that I knew I had to do something."

202

Mrs. Tubbs started to cry. "What would it've hurt?" she whined.

"You wouldn't know, would you?" Mrs. Ben said. "You wouldn't know on account of you're nothing but poor white trash from the creek bottom. What would it have hurt? I'll tell you what. Suppose they'd have come up with a kid with two heads or an idiot, or something. What would people say? Not that you'd care—you people more than likely marry your uncles all the time. You probably don't think a thing about it."

"So you killed him," Biggie said, looking square at her. "You hid in the kitchen until Firman was alone, and you shot him through the head."

Mrs. Ben didn't say a word, just stared at Biggie.

Biggie continued. "I'm guessing that when you left by the back door, you tossed the gun at the open Dumpster, only you missed."

Mrs. Ben nodded, looking down at the table.

"Was that when Clovis Threadgill came riding up?"

Mrs. Ben nodded again. "Before I could pick it up to chunk it in, that old fool had grabbed it and stuck it in his belt. He just looked at me and rode on off."

"So you decided he had to be silenced," Biggie said. "You drove out to his house pretending to take him a pie, and when you got your chance, you shot him, too. Did you think you'd killed him?"

"I knew he'd die soon enough," Mrs. Ben snarled. "Nobody ever goes around there."

I thought about Clovis lying in his dirty old bed alone and shot and not even being able to get himself a drink of water. Suddenly I wanted to get away from these women.

I wanted to go back to our house where Willie Mae was cooking supper and the Christmas tree lights were on and Booger was probably asleep on my pillow.

"So," Biggie said, "you killed Firman, then you killed Clovis because he saw—but why did you come after Billie Faye here? What changed your arrangement with her?"

"It was Ben," Mrs. Birdsong said. "Right after Firman died, he started getting fancy ideas. Started talking plans for expansion—new broiler houses, processing plants, another restaurant over in Center Point. He said we'd have to cut our personal spending, that Firman had played fast and loose with the money but now things would be different. Now he, Mister Bigwig, was going to put Fresh-as-a-Daisy on the map. He said he'd show Tyson and Pilgrim a thing or two about chickens. He was going to be the biggest chicken man in the South. Only thing was, I wasn't going to have any money to spend. Well, I sure as heck wasn't going to give what little I had to this hussy." She frowned and rubbed the back of her neck, then smiled an ugly smile. "Killing ain't so hard after the first time."

"Laverne," Biggie said, "you know you are going to have to go to jail, don't you?"

Mrs. Ben hung her head. "I'm thirsty. Could I have a glass of ice water?"

Mrs. Tubbs started to get up to get it, but Mrs. Ben beat her to it. "It's okay," she said. "I know where it is."

She walked slow toward the kitchen, and her rubber tennis shoes squeaked on the polished floor. As she headed toward the refrigerator, Biggie motioned for Rosebud to follow.

With her hand on the refrigerator door, Mrs. Ben glanced our way and then, quicker than grease, she flew out the back door and headed for her car. Rosebud was right behind her, but she had a head start. She had the big black Suburban going and spun out of the driveway, spraying gravel behind her.

In a flash, Biggie was on the phone to the police. She explained what had happened and told Paul and Silas to call the Highway Patrol and the Sheriff's Department to help look for Mrs. Ben. When she hung up, she called Fairy Lee to come over and stay with her mother until Mrs. Ben was locked up safe and sound. Mrs. Tubbs went to the kitchen and poured herself a glass of water. She drank it standing at the sink, looking out the window.

"Ya'll can go on home now," she said. "I'm gonna lay down and rest awhile."

When we got home, Biggie went upstairs to take a nap.

"Wake me up if Paul and Silas calls," she said. "He has all the officers in the area looking for her. They'll bring her in before night."

"I won't be here, Biggie," I said. "I've got to do my Christmas shopping."

I took my money out of the sock I kept it in and rode my old bike down to the square. It was near suppertime before I got my shopping done. I put my presents under the tree and went to the kitchen. Paul and Silas was sitting at the table with Biggie drinking a cup of coffee.

"So she's locked up safe and sound?" Biggie asked.

"Absolutely, Cousin Biggie. Ben's hired Rex Able from

over in Mount Pleasant to represent her. He's the best lawyer we've got around here. Naturally, Ben's griping about how much money it's going to cost."

"Naturally," Biggie said.

After Paul and Silas left, Biggie put her hands over her head and stretched. She gave a big, contented sigh. "Tomorrow's Christmas Eve," she said. "Let's all try and forget about crime—at least until the new year."

24

Booger woke me up Christmas morning by leaping right in the middle of my belly. Then he jumped onto the windowsill and meowed. I rolled over and looked out, and guess what—the ground was covered with snow, and more was falling in fat fluffy flakes.

I hurried up and put on my clothes and then knocked on Biggie's door. "Come on, Biggie. It's snowing!"

Next, I ran out back to Rosebud and Willie Mae's little house. I pounded on the door and yelled for Rosebud, then ran away on account of I didn't know how Willie Mae would take being waked up like that.

Rosebud stuck his head out the door and called me just as I was rounding the side of the house. "Get back inside. You ain't even got your coat on."

For the first time, I noticed I was a little chilly, so I went in the back door to find Biggie at the stove making coffee.

"First, we'll open presents," she said. "Then you can play in the snow all you want while Willie Mae and I fix Christmas dinner."

I got four video games, a new Dallas Cowboys jacket, a Batman watch, and a brand-new Dyno VFR bike just like the one those Culpeppers took back to Montana. Biggie said she liked the necklace and earring set I got her at Bob's Dollar Store, and Rosebud lit up one of the cigars I bought him right then and there. He said they were his favorite brand.

"Open yours, Willie Mae," I said. "You're really gonna like what I got you."

And she did. I got Willie Mae a brand-new pair of gold loop earrings to replace the ones Rosebud lost in a crap game. She gave me a big hug.

After the presents were all opened and me and Rosebud got through taking the wrappings and stuff to the garbage can, I went into the kitchen to see about dinner. Willie Mae was just taking a pan with a big turkey in it out of the oven.

"Ummm, smell that," Biggie said.

"I'm not eating any," I said, remembering how that bird had looked right at me like he was trying to say something. "I've decided to become a vegetarian."

Rosebud looked up from the table where he'd been chopping oranges and cranberries. "My oh me," he said. "Looks to me like I forgot all about one of your Christmas presents. Why don't we take a walk out to the garage?"

I didn't look at that turkey in the pan again, just followed him out the back door. When we got to the garage, I heard a funny sound. Rosebud pulled open the door, and I knew what it was. There, in a large cage, stood my turkey, the one we'd been fattening up out at Fresh-as-a-Daisy. He gobbled real loud and craned his neck at me, then went back to eating corn.

"Wow!"

"Whatcha gonna name him?" Rosebud asked.

"I don't know," I said, turning back toward the kitchen. "I wonder when dinner's gonna be ready. I might decide not to be a vegetarian after all."

Willie Mae's Aunt Nancy's Voodoo Beef Casserole

First, cook you up a medium-size package of egg noodles. (You can use more, if you've got company coming.) While your noodles are cooking, brown two pounds of good ground round in the skillet with a little oil. Add in a chopped onion. Now drain your noodles and pour your meat in on top. Next, you want to open two cans of Niblets corn, two eight-ounce cans of mushroom stems and pieces, two cans of RoTel tomatoes with green chili peppers, and one large can of tomatoes. (If you can't take the heat, better make that two cans of plain tomatoes and one can of RoTel.) Now pour all your vegetables into the meat and noodles WITH THE JUICE. That's what makes it good. Now open and drain two cans of pitted ripe olives. Cut um in half and add to the mixture. Pour the whole mess in a casserole dish (or two) and top with lots of good cheddar cheese. Bake at 375° until the cheese is melted and bubbly and beginning to brown a little around the edges.

This is good for the family, but if company's coming, I generally make up a salad of sliced avocados and grapefruit with poppy seed dressing.

M

Bell, Nancy,
1932-

Biggie and the
    fricasseed fat man.

$20.95

DATE			
20x			